at Dock
NORTH WING
HOUSE
SOUTH WING
Farm
LABORATORIES
CLIFF
SPINDRIFT ISLAND

Shanda Davidson

THE LOST CITY

The Rick Brant Science-Adventure *Stories*

BY JOHN BLAINE

The Rocket's Shadow
The Lost City
Sea Gold
100 Fathoms Under
The Whispering Box Mystery
The Phantom Shark
Smugglers' Reef
The Caves of Fear
Stairway to Danger
The Golden Skull
The Wailing Octopus
The Electronic Mind Reader
The Scarlet Lake Mystery
The Pirates of Shan
The Blue Ghost Mystery
The Egyptian Cat Mystery
The Flaming Mountain

Rick gripped Scotty's shoulder. "It's there! Scotty, I saw the antenna base."

THE LOST CITY

A RICK BRANT ELECTRONIC ADVENTURE

THE LOST CITY

By JOHN BLAINE

GROSSET & DUNLAP PUBLISHERS

NEW YORK, N. Y.

Printed in the United States of America

Contents

THE LOST CITY

CHAPTER I

Good-bye, Spindrift!

RICK BRANT put down his fork and refused a second helping of roast beef. It was good, but tonight he just wasn't hungry.

He looked at the faces around the big table and thought: "It'll be a long time before we're all together again."

He had been away from home before, but never for almost a whole year, and never without his father. Hartson Brant had to stay at Spindrift Island this time, to handle the home end of the experiment.

Rick's troubled eyes went from face to face. Next to him was Dr. Wisecarver, who would remain at home with Hartson Brant. On the doctor's other side was Professor Gordon. He would stay at home, too.

At the end of the table was his mother. She was smiling as she poured coffee for Professor Weiss, but Rick knew that she wasn't very happy about the coming expedition. His mother was a good sport, though. She hadn't made a single objection.

Julius Weiss, a meek-looking little man with just a fringe of hair on his head, was going along. Professor Weiss, Rick thought, looked more like a clerk or a bookkeeper than a noted mathematician. He seemed frail compared with good-natured Hobart Zircon, who sat next to him.

Professor Zircon was a huge barrel of a man, over six feet tall, with a bushy shock of hair and a voice that shook the walls. He was one of the country's foremost electronic scientists, and almost as famous as Rick's father.

"It will be fun," Rick thought, "having Zircon along." Where little Julius Weiss was inclined to be a worrybird and tart in his speech, Zircon was easygoing, and with a keen sense of humor.

Next to the big professor sat a tall, husky boy with black hair and a merry face. Rick told himself: "I wouldn't want to go if Scotty weren't going to be along."

Don Scott, called Scotty, was about Rick's own age, but he had three years of Marine Corps experience behind him. He had talked a recruiting sergeant into believing that he was of enlistment age, and had fought through the South Pacific and Central Pacific campaigns. In the months that Scotty had lived on Spindrift Island, he and Rick had become close friends. Closer than brothers, Rick thought, because brothers fight with each other sometimes, and Scotty and he never did.

The scrappy, humorous ex-marine had lived on Spindrift Island ever since he had rescued Rick from Manfred Wessel's gang before the launching of the moon rocket. Wessel, a renegade scientist, had tried to destroy the Spindrift rocket in order to launch one of his own and thus win the two-million-dollar Stoneridge Grant.

Scotty had been hired as an island guard, and he had helped Rick solve the rocket mystery and trap the Spindrift Island traitor who was helping Wessel. Since then, the Brants had accepted Scotty as one of them, and he was treated like a member of the family and not an employee.

Rick's eyes went to his sister, and he smiled. Barby Brant, a very pretty girl a year younger than Rick, was pecking at her food, a petulant expression on her face. He knew why: Barby had hoped all along that her parents would allow her to go on the expedition. Not until tonight had she accepted defeat.

At the head of table sat Hartson Brant. The famed electronic scientist felt his son's eyes upon him and he looked up and gave Rick a comradely wink.

Rick swallowed hard. He didn't like the idea of going halfway around the world without his father. To him, Hartson Brant was more than a famous scientist; he was a swell guy who could always find time for a fishing excursion, and who would put aside his own important work for a while, to help his son on some gadget he was working on.

Rick looked down at his plate, almost wishing that he had not asked to go. When a guy had such a swell family it was kind of dopey to go wandering off like this.

Then Barby spoke up and broke the silence that had hung so heavy over the dinner table.

"Rick, you won't forget to bring me a lama, will you?"

The laughter that followed dispelled the gloom.

"You're a little mixed up, towhead," Rick replied. "You're thinking of llamas—with two 'l's.' They're South American animals. A lama is a Tibetan priest, and I don't think one of them would want to come back with us as a souvenir for a girl."

"Even a pretty girl," Zircon added.

Barby rewarded the big professor with a smile. "Well," she said to Rick, "don't forget to bring me something."

Hartson Brant rose from the table. "Let's take our coffee out to the sun porch," he invited.

The family and the scientists carried their coffee cups out to the big porch, glassed in now, because it was still early spring. Beyond the porch, the seaward end of Spindrift Island fell away to the surf below. To the right, the long line of the laboratory buildings loomed against the night sky. And from the seaward end, a massive frame was silhouetted against a full moon.

Hobart Zircon pointed to it. "Symbolic," he boomed. "A full moon and the radar antenna."

"A good omen," Hartson Brant agreed. "I think we can take it as such."

Rick looked at the big antenna, or "bedspring," as it had been dubbed by Scotty. A long time from now that intricate frame would send radar impulses hurtling toward the moon, to be reflected back to the other side of the earth, where he, Scotty, Zircon, and Weiss would be waiting.

Barby spoke up. "I don't see why they have to go all the way to Tibet! Why can't you bounce your old message back to . . . to Whiteside?"

Whiteside was the little town nearest them on the New Jersey mainland. The scientists smiled, and Hartson Brant explained: "It wouldn't quite suit our purpose, Barby." He pointed to the moon. "That piece of green cheese up there is the top of a triangle. Spindrift Island is another corner. We've chosen a plateau in Tibet for the third corner because it's just about the most distant point we could find."

"And for a good many other sound, scientific reasons," Julius Weiss added. "No, my dear, I'm afraid Whiteside just wouldn't do."

"If it were Whiteside," said Barby, "I could go, too. Why did I have to be a girl?" she mourned.

"You wouldn't like Tibet," Scotty said. "Nothing but rocks, and mountains and snow."

"I doubt that we'll see a great deal of snow," Hobart Zircon remarked. "We've chosen the time of year when travel in Tibet is easiest. We'll see snow, of course, on the mountaintops. But I don't think we'll have to wade through any."

Rick sat back quietly, listening to the conversation. He didn't feel much like talking. He didn't want to acknowledge that the gnawing feeling inside of him was homesickness, but he knew it was. Homesick already? The feeling would leave, once they were under way.

Scotty was saying: ". . . I'm dense, I guess, but I still don't know just what it'll prove even if we do bounce a message off the moon from here to Tibet and back."

"Just another attempt to make the world smaller, Scotty," Hartson Brant said. "At present, world-wide communications are very poor, at least in remote places. Telegraph wires aren't practical over too great distances, and radio depends too much on local atmospheric conditions. If we can use the moon for a relay point and bounce messages from place to place without interference, we may solve the communications problem."

"At least, the International Communications Association thinks so," Dr. Wisecarver said. "They're backing the experiment by setting up listening points all over the world. It's a pretty important thing, son."

"I guess it is," Scotty acknowledged.

Mrs. Brant rose. "It's getting late. Hadn't you all better finish your packing? I'll have a snack ready when you're through."

The gathering broke up, and Rick and Scotty went upstairs to their rooms.

"Not talking much tonight, Rick," Scotty commented.

"I don't feel like it," he admitted. "With you it's different. You saw the world when you were in the Marines, but I've never been so far from home before."

"I feel the same way," Scotty answered. "It didn't matter much, before, because I didn't have any folks.

But now . . ." His voice trailed off and he went into his own room.

Nothing remained but their personal gear. All the equipment for the experiment had been crated and sent to New York, all their trail stuff was packed, including army-type rations, sleeping bags, and anything else they might need.

The workbench Rick had built into one wall of his room was open, and he went to it, picking up the compact little gadget that lay there. He hefted it in his hand. "Might as well take it along. If things get dull I can do a little work on it," he mused.

Around the walls were other gadgets. He disconnected them sadly, wondering when they would be used again. There was his automatic window closer and heat control, his electric snack bar for making sandwiches when the rest of the family was asleep, the old leather armchair he had wired up for reading.

People meeting Rick Brant for the first time found it hard to believe that he already had an excellent grasp of the electronic sciences. He looked as though he might have a better acquaintance with a football field or a tennis court than with an electrical laboratory, because he was tall for his age, and huskily built. He had brown hair and brown eyes, and his face was always tanned, even in winter, since he was out of doors so much. His personal experiments and the work he did, as an apprentice to his famous father, had never interfered with his love of sports.

While he was at work with his screw driver, Barby

came in and sat on the bed, her pert face thoughtful. Rick looked up and smiled at her.

"What's the matter, towhead? Still sulking because you can't go with us?"

"Pooh, who wants to go to Tibet?" retorted Barby. But she was in no mood for teasing tonight. "Rick, you and Scotty will be careful, won't you?" she asked soberly.

"Sure, sis," Rick replied gently. "Don't worry about us."

"I will worry. I'm afraid, Rick."

"About us? Don't be silly," Rick returned affectionately. It wasn't like Barby to worry. She usually had supreme confidence in the ability of Rick and Scotty to take care of themselves.

She bounced off the bed. "Gosh, I almost forgot! I have packages for both of you."

Scotty came in as she left. "What's Barby up to?"

"She forgot something," Rick told him.

In a moment Barby was back with two packages, both wrapped in heavy oiled paper and sealed with tape. Scotty's was about six inches square and eighteen inches long. Rick's was a square about twelve inches on a side.

Handing the packages to the boys, she said, "You're not supposed to open them until the Fourth of July."

Rick held his up to his ear and shook it. It didn't rattle. "Aren't you going to tell us what's in them?"

"No," Barby answered. "You'll open them on the Fourth, and then you'll think of us back here."

"We'll think of you anyway," Scotty assured her. "Both of us are a little homesick already."

Barby's blue eyes suddenly filled with tears. She swallowed hard and said, "Don't forget to be careful, please!"

Rick was at her side. "Hey, towhead! What is this?"

"I'm afraid. My . . . my intuition tells me something awful is going to happen."

Rick's eyes met Scotty's across the top of the girl's golden head.

"We'll be careful," Scotty promised seriously.

"Sure, sis," Rick said, "And thanks for the packages. We'll send you something nice from Bombay."

Barby brightened. "Really, Rick? What?"

"I don't know yet," he replied, grinning. "Maybe a white elephant."

"I guess it'll be more fun if you surprise me," she said gravely. Then, with a smile for both of them, "I better go help Mother."

Rick started checking over his camera case as she went out the door. When her rapid footsteps had retreated down the hall, he looked up at Scotty and shook his head.

"Funny. It isn't like Barby to be afraid. She doesn't usually let her imagination run away with her."

"She did this time," Scotty said.

Rick counted film packs thoughtfully. Barby had a lot of wild ideas, but she had sense, too. She didn't ordinarily jump at shadows. "But maybe her hunch is right," he said. "Maybe this trip isn't going to be as easy as it looks."

Later, as they walked across the orchard, Rick and Scotty looked around at all the old familiar things, each wondering when they would see them again.

Barby held tight to Rick's hand and asked questions, while Dismal, Rick's shaggy pup, raced ahead, then back to their sides.

"Rick, why aren't you going on a big ship—like the *Queen Mary* or something? An old freighter will be awful."

"Not so bad," Rick said. "We'll be the only passengers. Dad fixed passage so we could stay with the equipment. We couldn't have done that on a regular passenger ship."

"Besides," Scotty added, "this ship goes right to Bombay."

They came out of the orchard onto the grassy strip at the seaward side of the island. In the moonlight, the slim shape of a little airplane gleamed silver.

A lump came into Rick's throat. One of his true loves was his Piper Cub airplane. It was strange to think that he wouldn't be flying again for almost a year. The Cub would be used, though. Professor Gordon had been a navy pilot before he turned to science, and he would be doing the island's errands.

Rick turned away from the Cub and led the way to the laboratory building. He looked around him, seeing the workbenches, the big racks with their complex amplifiers, the door to the power room, the door to the radiation room. But he didn't stop to examine anything closely. He headed for the stairs that led to the roof.

It was up here that Professor Weiss had watched the moon rocket through his telescope. And now it was up here that the big radar antenna rested.

Rick went over to its shadow, Barby and Scotty walking silently beside him. They looked out over Spindrift Island.

There were lights in the house, and lights in the farmhouse back on the north side, but the rest of the island was dark. Rick saw the gleam of the dismantled rocket launcher in Pirate's Field, and the darkness of the woods beyond. He looked past the house toward the boat landing from which they would leave in the morning, and a lump came up into his throat again.

Dismal brushed against his leg and whined for attention. Rick bent over and patted him, and the shaggy pup rolled over and played dead. This was his only trick, and he performed it at every opportunity.

"Let's go back to the house," the boy said gruffly.

CHAPTER II

Sabotage

THE *John S. Madigan* wasn't the last word in comfort, but it was adequate. The four travelers shared the only passenger cabin, Rick and Scotty sleeping in the two upper bunks, the professors taking the lowers.

Rick was conscious of a growing excitement as the ship breasted the Atlantic swells and they reviewed the myriad details of the expedition.

Everything had been worked out in advance, of course, but the two professors spent considerable time rechecking their data, and Rick and Scotty were given the task of rechecking supplies, just to be sure they had everything. In such a major undertaking, even little details were too important to be forgotten.

Rick ran to Professor Zircon one day. "Sir, I can't find maps on any of the lists. We'll need maps, won't we?"

"That's all arranged," Zircon told him. "Our maps are being prepared by the Asiatic Geographical Union in Bombay. They have experts who know Tibet intimately. We'll pick up the maps there."

Julius Weiss looked up from the volume he was studying. "Rick, have you gone down to look at the equipment today?"

"Why, no, sir, I haven't."

"Please do," Weiss said querulously. "We must keep a careful watch on it."

"Why, Julius?" Zircon bellowed.

"How do I know? I just think it would be a good idea," the little professor replied testily.

"I'll look at the stuff," Rick promised.

Weiss had been growing more and more worried about details. He had asked Rick and Scotty to recheck the supply lists several times, finally looking at them himself.

"What is that you're reading, sir?" Rick asked. The volume interested him. It was written in a script he had never seen before.

"I'm brushing up on my Tamil," Weiss answered.

Zircon grunted. "But we won't be in the Tamil country, Julius. Tamil is spoken largely in the south of India and in Ceylon."

"I enjoy studying," Weiss said shortly.

Zircon winked at Rick as the little professor went back to the book. Languages were one of Weiss's hobbies—his most important hobby, in fact. As soon as he heard a new tongue spoken he had to try to learn it. Rick knew that he spoke French, German, Spanish,

Italian, and Portuguese with native fluency. Zircon had told him that Weiss also spoke quite good Mandarin, Chinese, Mongol, Malay, and Japanese. He also knew a smattering of strange, local dialects like the Tagalog of the Philippines.

As Rick went out to the deck, where Scotty was taking a sun bath, he shook his head and grinned. It was hard to imagine little Julius Weiss as an adventurer who had covered the Pacific in his youth, but he had Zircon's word for it that Weiss had been quite a traveler.

Scotty squinted up at him as he approached. "Relax, friend. Stretch out and take advantage of the ultraviolet rays."

"You're a vegetable, Sergeant Scott," Rick said. "You're a turnip. You just lie still and get warm in the sun. Don't you realize this is a great adventure? Get up and look at the sea."

"I saw a wave once," Scotty murmured comfortably. He rolled over on his stomach. "Go away. I hate people who aren't lazy."

Rick left him to his slumbers and went up on the bridge. Captain Marks greeted him cordially. "Getting restless, son? We're off the Azores right now." He indicated the position on the chart. "Won't be long before we're steaming into the Mediterranean."

"I always thought going to sea was exciting, Captain Marks. But it's just sailing on, day after day. The scenery never changes," Rick remarked.

The captain smiled. "Oh, I don't know. Scenery

isn't so much. It's the unexpected that makes for adventure, I'd say, and there's plenty of that on the sea."

"Plenty of it in Tibet, too, I guess," Rick said.

The first officer came up to consult the captain so Rick left, still feeling restless. The days were growing monotonous. He passed the radio room and glanced in and saw the racks of equipment.

An idea hit him. His little gadget! Why not pass a few hours working on it? He had to think for a minute before he could remember where it was. He had put it in with the trail gear, in one of the wooden crates. It was down in the hold.

Professor Weiss had asked him to look over the equipment. He could kill two birds at once. He went down the accommodation ladder to the next deck and made his way forward through the passages till he came to the huge watertight door of the hold. It was dogged down. He had to struggle with some of the heavy metal fastenings before he could open it. Then he stepped inside and fumbled for the light switch.

The lights snapped on and he saw boxes of goods stacked all around him. He knew where their own equipment was; he had checked off the crates as they were stowed. He made his way to them, sniffing in the stale air a sharp, acrid odor.

He reached the first of the cases stenciled *Stoneridge Expedition* and noticed that the odor was stronger and that part of the stencil was obliterated by a brown streak.

"Funny," he muttered. "Something's leaking."

Then his eyes opened wide as he saw the box which had been placed carefully on the very top of the pile. It was on its side!

He ran to the door of the hold, yelling at the top of his lungs. "Help, someone!"

Just outside the door was a fire extinguisher, of the soda and acid type. Working furiously, he unscrewed the ringed top and tossed it aside. The bottle of acid was in its pivoted cradle. He lifted it out and placed it cautiously on the deck, then he took the big metal container of soda solution and lugged it back to the equipment as fast as he could.

Holding the container high over his head, he let the solution cascade down over the boxes. Instantly there was a sputter and the solution foamed in a great yellow mass.

The container was empty now. Rick ran for another, and met a member of the crew who had come in answer to his yell.

"Get the captain," Rick shouted.

"What's up?" the sailor demanded.

"Acid!" Rick yelled at him. "There's acid all over our equipment!"

CHAPTER III

Fire in the Hold

UNDER Captain Marks's efficient direction, the acid was quickly neutralized with soda solution rushed from the galley. Then, as seamen set to work cleaning up the mess, the captain turned to Rick, Scotty, and the professors.

"Now," he said, "let's get down to cases. Where did that acid come from?"

"It's battery acid, sir," Rick answered. "We had a carboy of it for our batteries—the ones we use for heating the tube filaments."

Professor Zircon had been examining the empty container. "The acid bottle was firmly sealed and placed upright in this weighted box," he explained. "It would have been almost impossible for it to spill. Even if it had fallen on its side, the acid still would not have run out."

"But it did," Julius Weiss remarked tartly. "How do you explain that?" He was examining the crates one at a time, anxiously searching for signs of damage. "We'll have to rip these crates open," he said.

Captain Marks bent over and examined the acid container. Presently the skipper straightened up. "It would be hard for it to tip over," he admitted, "but there's no other answer. The crates must have been badly piled. My guess is that they shifted a bit, just enough to tip the acid crate."

"But how could it come unstoppered?" Rick objected.

The skipper shrugged. "Very possibly it wasn't as tightly sealed as you thought. Fortunately you found it before much damage was done. I'll lend you a man to help inspect the crates, and I can supply another carboy of acid from my own stores."

He motioned to a thickset man near by. "Chips, bear a hand here." To Zircon he added, "This is Meekin, the ship's carpenter. He'll help you with the crates. Now, if you'll excuse me, I'll get back to the bridge."

Julius Weiss was alternately trying to get into the stacked cases and wringing his hands. "I'm sure something is ruined!" he exclaimed. "If the acid reached the cathode units, Hobart, I'm afraid we're ruined! Ruined!"

"Nonsense," Zircon bellowed. "Rick found the trouble too soon for much to have happened." He turned to the boy. "That was fast thinking, using the soda from the extinguisher."

Rick blushed, and turned to lend a hand in shifting crates. He hadn't even stopped to think. He had acted instinctively.

Scotty helped him with a large crate and spoke softly

so that the professors couldn't hear. "What do you think?"

"Think about what?"

"The acid. Does it look like an accident to you?"

Rick gave the crate a final heave. "What are you driving at, Scotty? It has to be an accident." Just the same, there was an uneasy feeling growing in him.

"Why does it have to be an accident?" Scotty insisted. "You got into the hold. Anyone else could have."

"But why should they? This isn't like the moon rocket, Scotty. No one could gain anything by trying to stop this experiment, and people don't do things without reason."

"But that acid container was designed specially so it *wouldn't* tip over," Scotty persisted.

"Yes, but if the pile shifted . . ."

"It still wouldn't tip over. It would slide down."

Scotty had put into words the very thing that had been at the back of Rick's mind. It was true. The wooden container that held the acid bottle was heavily weighted at the base. It would take a real effort to tip it.

"I can't imagine why anyone would want to sabotage the equipment," Rick said thoughtfully. "I think maybe some sailor was working down here and tipped it over accidentally. The acid started pouring out and he got scared and beat it."

"Maybe," Scotty replied doubtfully.

With the help of Meekin, the professors were already

probing into the crates, to see if any acid might have seeped through onto the equipment. In one or two spots they found marks where the powerful acid had started to eat into the aluminum cases that housed the delicate radar gear. But by applying the fire extinguisher so quickly, Rick had prevented the acid from eating all the way through.

He and Scotty bore a hand to lift one particularly heavy crate that was nothing but a framework of boards. Inside, clearly visible, was a cast-aluminum pyramid that looked like an oversize automobile jack.

"The stuff didn't touch the antenna base," he said.

Under the professor's direction, Meekin tore open crates and nailed them up again. He was a sullen man of middle age who evidently resented having to do this extra work.

Rick searched until he found the box which contained his gadget. The box was hinged, and closed with a snap lock. He opened it, disclosing neatly packed sleeping bags, windbreakers, rain hoods, ponchos, and similar stuff to be used on the trail. Under the jackets was the little aluminum box he wanted. He tucked it into his pocket.

The last traces of acid had been neutralized, and the inspection was at an end. Rick joined Scotty and the professors as they walked out of the hold, leaving the carpenter to lock the door behind them.

"How did you happen to arrive at the right moment, Rick?" Zircon asked.

Rick produced the metal box and held it up. "I was after this."

Weiss peered at it in the dim light below decks. "What is it?"

"The most important radio device since the vacuum tube," Rick boasted jokingly. He put it back into his pocket. "I'll show it to you when I've done a little more work on it."

As they came out on deck, Weiss shook his head. "Hobart, I don't like this. It's a bad start, having that container tip like that for no reason. I've been afraid something like this would happen."

"Baseless fears," Zircon snorted. "I'm surprised at you, Julius."

"Not baseless," Weiss contradicted. "We have overlooked necessary detail, Hobart. We have been remiss. I am sure of it."

"What detail have we overlooked?" Zircon demanded. "Our equipment has been checked time and again. Our travel permissions are arranged. The passports are in my pocket. Our maps are being checked in Bombay at this moment. What detail, Julius?"

"We haven't arranged for guides," Weiss declared triumphantly.

"Certainly not. Hartson Brant and I discussed that. We decided that it would be wiser and less expensive to pick up a native guide at the Tibetan frontier."

The two professors walked toward their cabin, still wrangling. Rick and Scotty stopped at the rail.

Rick shook his head. "Professor Weiss is as full of worries as my Aunt Jennifer. I didn't think he'd be like this."

"He has a lot on his mind," Scotty said. "This experiment means everything to him. Remember, he worked out all the transmission details."

"I know," Rick admitted. "But he shouldn't worry about every little thing."

"He'll worry until we take down the message from Spindrift on July tenth," Scotty answered. "Now, come on, guy, let's see that super invention of yours."

Rick grinned. "Super isn't the word. It's positively atomic." He took the metal box from his pocket. It was very tiny, not larger than two cigarette packages. He opened the lid and passed the box to Scotty.

Inside was an intricate arrangement of wires, resisters, tubes, and condensers.

"My gosh, look at those tubes! They're no bigger than . . . than acorns!" Scotty exclaimed.

"That's what they're called. Acorn tubes."

"But what's it for?"

Rick eyed the neat little set proudly. "Well, I read in the paper a while back about a kid who rigged up a receiving set in his hat."

"In his hat?"

"Helmet, rather. You know . . . one of those sun helmets. So I thought I'd go him one better and see if I could figure out a transceiver . . ."

"A what?"

"A set that transmits as well as receives. Then we could each have one, and we could send messages back and forth. See?"

"Yes," Scotty marveled. "But why should we send messages back and forth? We're together all the time. And this wouldn't work at long range, would it?"

"Don't get practical," Rick replied. "I was just figuring it out for the fun of it. We might find a use for it someday."

The skipper came by, on his way down from the bridge, and stopped. "Hungry, boys? Chow is down."

"That's for me," Scotty said.

As they fell in step, Rick asked, "Captain, was anyone in the hold earlier today?"

The skipper looked at him curiously. "Not to my knowledge. Why?"

"I just wondered if perhaps the acid was knocked over accidentally by someone who went into the hold."

"I'll ask the mates, but I doubt that anyone was in the hold. I think your acid spilled over when the crates shifted. Improper stowage caused it. If I find the man responsible, he'll regret it. I will not tolerate carelessness on my ship."

Rick let the matter drop, but he was not satisfied. Shifting cargo was too pat an answer. Still, there was no other explanation. He would just have to accept it. Fortunately, no damage had been done.

After dinner, he went to work on the little radio unit, working with such delicate tools as a pair of tweezers and a jeweler's screw driver. Scotty sat on the opposite bunk cleaning his rifle with loving care. To the ex-marine, weapons were holy things. He inspected the rifle every day, running an oily rag through the barrel and wiping off the mechanism.

"Someday you're going to take one of those things apart and not be able to get it back together again," Rick teased.

Scotty grinned good-naturedly. "Stick to your gimmicks and leave the shootin' irons to me, son." He held the rifle barrel up to the light and peered through it. "Like a mirror," he said with satisfaction.

It was a beautiful weapon, a present to Scotty from Hartson Brant. Scotty had added a telescopic sight. With that and his marine training, plus the high power of the rifle—it was .303 caliber—he could break a dinner plate at better than five hundred yards. Rick had seen him do it.

"Hope we won't need that," he remarked.

"We won't," Scotty said optimistically. "But maybe I'll get a shot at a wild goat, or maybe a panda."

When Zircon and Weiss came in, the boys climbed up to their bunks. Scotty put his rifle into its canvas case, and Rick put his little radio set on the cabin desk. They undressed quickly and got into bed.

In a little while Zircon snapped out the lights and there was silence in the cabin. The ship pitched slightly to the swell, a slow, soothing motion that made Rick's eyelids droop.

Just before he dozed off, he asked sleepily, "Scotty, why would anyone want to stop the experiment?"

Hobart Zircon answered for Scotty, his voice loud in the darkness. "No one would, Rick. Go to sleep and stop worrying about it."

"Yes, sir," Rick said. He punched his pillow into a more comfortable shape, and after a while he slept.

It was shortly after midday of the next day that Rick made another discovery. The morning had been spent on the foredeck, sun bathing and chatting with the professors and Scotty. Not until after lunch did he feel bored and decide to go back to his work on the radio set.

It wasn't on the cabin desk where he had left it.

He hunted through the cabin, through their baggage, even under the bunk mattresses. Then he hurried out to Scotty and the professors, who were leaning against the rail.

"Did any of you take my radio unit?"

There were three negative answers.

"Someone did," he insisted. "I left it in the cabin and it's gone."

"You undoubtedly mislaid it," Professor Weiss said.

"No, sir. I looked everywhere. It's not there."

"He left it on the desk," Scotty remembered. "Just before we went to bed last night."

"It will turn up, Rick," Zircon boomed. "Surely no one would steal it."

"It wouldn't do them any good," Rick replied. "It doesn't work." He left his friends and hurried to the bridge.

Captain Marks greeted him cordially. "Something on your mind? You look worried."

"My radio unit is gone," Rick blurted out. He told the skipper about it, adding, "It must have been taken. It isn't in the cabin."

Captain Marks rubbed his chin. "You're sure of that? I don't want to start something and then have it turn up under your bunk."

"I searched every inch of our cabin, sir," Rick said.

The skipper shook his head. "I hate to think we have a thief aboard. I'll have the first mate talk to the crew, one at a time. It would do no good to search the ship. Too many places it could be hidden. You say it's of no value?"

"To no one but me, sir. It's just a gadget I was working on."

At supper that night Captain Marks reported: "Not a thing doing, Rick. The crew denies all knowledge of it. I'm afraid it's gone for good unless it just happens to turn up somewhere."

"I put in a lot of work on it," Rick lamented. "Now I'll have to wait until we get home before I can start again, because we haven't the parts here."

"Never mind," Zircon soothed him. "We have a nice big radar transmitter for you to play with until we get back."

Rick looked at him sharply and saw the twinkle in the big professor's eyes. "It's not the same thing," he said. "This was my pet project. The radar transmitter is yours."

"You can have a share," Zircon suggested.

Rick fell silent, but the loss of his toy rankled. Anyway, he thought, whoever stole it won't get much out of it. It was a long way from being finished.

In the excitement of passing through the Mediterranean, the loss of the little transceiver was forgotten by everyone but Rick.

When they stopped at Port Said to refuel the ship, the boys had their first look at a foreign port. But there was no chance to go ashore, so they had to content themselves with watching from the deck. The professors, both experienced travelers, had been in the colorful port before and didn't think much of it.

"They said we didn't miss much," Rick said regretfully as the ship steamed between the narrow banks of the Suez Canal, "but I still wish we could have gotten ashore for a little while."

The passage through the canal passed without incident and the freighter plowed into the Indian Ocean. The heat was like a wet, heavy blanket now, and sleep was almost impossible. But the party looked forward eagerly to Bombay.

"Can't be soon enough," Scotty remarked as they climbed into the bunks one night. "I want a look at this India."

"Same here," Rick answered. He swung into the upper bunk, careful not to step on the professor below him.

He stretched out, only a sheet over him, and soon drifted off into a dreamland peopled with natives who wore cloth-of-gold trappings and turbans, and where elephants roamed the streets at will.

Then suddenly he jerked awake, and sat bolt upright, his ears filled with the ear-splitting clang of the alarm bell!

All four of the party leaped off their bunks, and Zircon snapped on the lights just as the third officer ran by.

"Fire!" he shouted. "All hands! Fire in the forward hold!"

CHAPTER IV

A Man Named Conway

RICK beat Scotty to the hold by about a yard and stopped short. "The equipment!" he exclaimed in horror.

Seamen were directing the streams from the extinguishers and sea hoses into the hold right at the precious radar gear. Overhead, the hatch was being lifted so that more water could be poured in.

Smoke curled out, mixed with steam. Captain Marks came out through the smoke, blackened and red-eyed. "Cut down on that water!" he yelled hoarsely. "Cut it down! It's nothing but smoke."

Professor Weiss grabbed Rick's arm. "The equipment! Rick, do something!"

"Nothing he can do," Hobart Zircon bellowed. "It's up to the captain and the crew."

"We *are* ruined this time, Hobart. Do you hear?" Weiss was on the verge of hysteria.

Rick and Scotty pressed close to the door, forgetting they were in pajamas and bare feet. Through the swirling smoke they could see shadowy piles of cargo, and they knew their equipment was in there where the smoke was thickest.

"Professor Weiss is right. This finishes us, Scotty," Rick said huskily.

He had a swift vision of his father's face, and those of the other scientists, when they heard the news. Months of preparation had gone up in smoke in that blackened hold.

Captain Marks pushed by him into the hold again, shouting, "All right, get that hatch off. Smartly, now! Let's get this smoke out of here."

Rick was at his heels, feeling the blast of fresh air as the big hatch cover on deck finally came off. Someone threw a switch and the hold was flooded with light from emergency lamps, the smoke eddying upward in the draft of air.

Rick pushed his way to the equipment, ankle-deep in dirty water and floating debris. He turned to find Scotty behind him.

"Over here," he motioned. The stacked equipment was charred and dirty. A lump came into Rick's throat, and his eyes watered with something more than smoke irritation. "What a mess!" He shook his head sadly.

"Wait a minute," Scotty said. "Maybe it isn't so bad." He was already lifting crates off the top of the pile, examining them on all sides.

"Look, Rick, the outer ones are charred a little, but most of them are okay. They're all wet, though."

Rick jumped to help him, his hopes rising. "The wetness doesn't matter. They have waterproof plastic linings. Come on, Scotty, let's dig!"

The professors were with them now, and they worked frantically, unstacking the crates, looking anxiously for signs of damage.

Zircon straightened up from his inspection of a bulky wooden box. "Thank God," he said. "The radio-frequency oscillator unit is undamaged."

Beside him, Weiss pounced on another crate. "The modulator!" He looked it over feverishly. "Not burned. Hobart, what good fortune!"

Captain Marks appeared beside them. "How bad is it?"

"Possibly not hopeless," Zircon replied. "We'll have to get the crates out on deck and open them to really tell."

"We'll do that right away," the captain said, "after we find out what started this. There's nothing combustible down here. Most of the cargo is toolmaking machinery."

The skipper and the first officer began a careful inspection of the hold. Scotty and Rick followed, watching curiously as they looked for the origin of the fire.

Right behind the stack of scientific equipment, Scotty bent down and picked up a charred rag. "Holy smoke!" he exclaimed. "Look at this!"

The ship's officers and Rick hurried to his side. The rag smelled strongly of kerosene.

Captain Marks and the mate exchanged glances.

"Sabotage," the captain said sharply. "It looks like the fire was set right next to your gear, Rick."

A thread of fear went through him.

Professor Weiss had been exploring a stack of cases beyond the equipment. Suddenly he let out a hoarse yell.

"Look! There's a dead man here!"

Instantly all hands were running to him. Captain Marks bent over the limp form lying behind the cases.

"He's not dead. Someone help me get him up."

Scotty took hold of the man's shoulders and they lifted him to a near-by crate.

Rick saw that it was the ship's carpenter, Meekin, his mouth open and his eyes closed. He was breathing, but with quick, shallow breaths.

"Let's get him into the air," the skipper urged. Willing hands lifted the prostrate form and carried him up the ladders to the deck.

In the open air, Meekin stirred feebly and tried to sit up, looking around him with dazed eyes.

"There's your saboteur," Scotty said.

There was a hint of dazed comprehension in the carpenter's face. "What happened, Chips?" Captain Marks grated.

Meekin coughed smoke from his lungs.

"You set the fire and the smoke got you before you could get out, isn't that it?"

Meekin coughed again.

The skipper shook him roughly. "No stalling. Wasn't that it?"

The carpenter looked up at the faces above him, at Professor Zircon's huge bulk, at Scotty's grim face, at Rick.

"Yeah," he said. "Yeah."

The first officer arrived with a bottle of brandy and poured the fiery stuff down the carpenter's mouth. Meekin coughed until his face was purple, but he recovered noticeably.

"Take him to the wardroom," the skipper directed two seamen. "We want to talk to him."

The officers gathered in the wardroom with the scientists and the two boys. Meekin, still weak but now able to talk coherently, sat in a chair and faced his accusers, his face sullen.

"Okay," he said. "Okay. I set the fire, but it was an accident."

"An accident, with rags soaked in kerosene? Don't hand us that stuff." Captain Marks's pleasant face was stern. "You could have burned the ship out from under us if the watch hadn't been on the job. Better talk, Meekin. And fast!"

"It was an accident," Meekin repeated thickly. "About the hold bein' open, I mean. I figgered if the hold was dogged down tight the fire wouldn't spread. It would maybe die from lack of air. But the smoke got me, like you said, and I passed out before I could get to the door."

"Why did you set the fire, Meekin?"

Rick moved closer, his eyes riveted to the man's streaked face.

"I had me orders," Meekin said at last.

"Who from?" Rick demanded.

The pale eyes went from face to face. "Suppose I don't talk?"

Captain Marks said slowly, "You almost destroyed this ship, Meekin. You almost left the crew and officers adrift in lifeboats, not to mention our passengers. You talk, or I'll let the rest of the crew persuade you."

Meekin paled under the coating of grime.

Rick's eyes went to the captain. He looked fully capable of carrying out the threat, though the boy was sure it was only a bluff.

But if it were, Meekin had no intention of calling it. "I got my orders from a guy named Conway," he said.

"How?"

"He telephoned me in New York. From Bombay. He said he'd give me a thousand bucks if I wrecked the equipment these guys were bringing aboard." He jerked his thumb at the professors.

"You spilled that bottle of acid," Rick accused him. "You tried to ruin the equipment that way first!"

Meekin's pale eyes met his. "You can't prove it," the carpenter continued hastily.

"We won't have to," the skipper shot back. "We've got you cold on this fire. Who is Conway?"

"He's a con man," Meekin said. "I knew him in China. He knew I was in the States, because I've kept in touch with him off and on. When he called, I knew he was good for the dough, so I agreed to do the job."

"But why did he want our equipment wrecked?" Professor Zircon barked.

Meekin shrugged. "That's his business."

"Talk," the skipper snapped.

"I can't! This guy called me on the telephone and said to work my connections to get on this ship and then get rid of the gear. That's all I know."

"Why did you steal my little radio?" Rick asked suddenly.

Meekin opened his mouth to speak then clamped it shut again.

"You thought it was part of the radar equipment," Rick continued. "Maybe an important part. So you stole it."

"I don't know what yer talkin' about," Meekin growled.

"Never mind," Weiss put in. "It isn't important, Rick. We can be sure he stole it, as you said, and probably threw it overboard. What is important is finding out why this Conway wanted our equipment sabotaged."

"I tell you I don't know!"

"I believe him," Captain Marks said. "Probably he was hired to do a job, without further explanations. Well, Meekin, I don't know what the maritime authorities will think about this, but you'll have a chance to find out."

He turned to the first mate. "We haven't a brig, unfortunately, but that gear locker by the forward companionway will do nicely. See that he's locked up."

To the scientists he said, "Now, gentlemen, let's have your gear on deck where we can look it over."

It was nearing dawn before the inspection was completed and the uncrated equipment stowed under canvas on the forward deck.

The professors had gone over it thoroughly and found a few ruined parts, but nothing—by a great stroke of fortune—that couldn't be replaced by any radio supply house. Professor Zircon radioed ahead to Bombay, requesting a British firm to have replacements ready.

Now all that remained was to recrate the stuff before Bombay was reached, and to unravel the mystery of Conway.

Dawn came as Rick and Scotty leaned on the rail and talked, watching the dark canal banks slip by.

"There's no answer," Rick concluded. "We know that a man named Conway wants to wreck our equipment, and that he'll pay big money to have it done. But we don't know who he is or why he wants to do it."

"It's creepy," Scotty answered. "We'll have to be on the watch from now on, without knowing who or what we're watching for."

"This equipment is mostly special stuff, you know," Rick said thoughtfully. "Dad and the rest put it together themselves, from their own designs. If it were lost, the expedition would have to stop until more could be made."

"How long would that take?"

"I don't know exactly. Months. Maybe six, maybe more."

"Then you figure someone wants to stop the expedition? But why?"

"Search me," Rick replied. "Maybe we'll find the answer in Bombay."

CHAPTER V

Bombay

THE blue of the Indian Ocean was fast turning to a muddy brown, a sign that they were nearing land. But the heat haze low over the water limited visibility to a few thousand feet.

Rick and Scotty were already packed, and the professors were below, collecting the last of their gear.

"The skipper said we should see land pretty soon," Rick said.

Scotty took his arm. "Look!"

Far ahead, swimming out of the mist, were sails. They shimmered in the heat haze, some of them red, some brown, some gaudy with patches of many colors.

The skipper came by and paused long enough to say: "Dhows. Native craft."

Rick and Scotty watched eagerly as the curved, graceful craft drew near. They forged past, and dark-skinned, turbaned men waved and yelled.

"Gosh, it's just like the movies, isn't it?" Scotty remarked. "All those colored sails and stuff. Reminds me of a travelogue I saw once."

Far ahead, a darker blur was visible through the heat haze. The boys watched in silence, eager for their first glimpse of India. Hobart Zircon joined them. He mopped his face with a huge handkerchief.

"Bombay," he rumbled. "I can smell it already."

Rick sniffed. Sure enough, there was a new odor in the air. It was pungent, spicy, rather unpleasant. But it was completely new, and he felt a pleasant tingle of anticipation.

Professor Weiss arrived, and they watched as India unfolded before them. Soon, large buildings were visible, some of them of white stone, some of brick. And then the docks themselves were in sight, and the ship was edging up to a pier next to a ship that flew the British ensign. One of the sailors threw a line that was caught by scantily clad men on the dock. The mooring line ran out, and they were secured.

Rick and Scotty watched, fascinated by the teeming throngs on the docks. All the dock equipment was modern: big cranes, concrete piers, railroad tracks close by. But the people were like something out of the *Arabian Nights*. The dock workers seemed to be all of a kind, all clad in brief, draped rags, and with soiled turbans on their heads.

The gangway was lowered to the dock, and the skipper shook hands all around.

"Well," he said with a hard smile, "we made it

There were a few moments when I had my doubts, thanks to our friend Meekin. I'm turning him in today."

Zircon and Weiss checked the baggage with customs officials while Rick and Scotty hurried up the ladder, eager for a closer look at the strange sights.

Over beneath a huge crane, a crowd had gathered. A boy was doing a juggling act with a handful of stones for the entertainment of some of the dock workers. Near by, gaunt old men crouched over huge bowls of foodstuffs which neither boy could identify. Their voices, cracked and shrill, lifted rhythmically as they hawked their wares.

Zircon and Weiss came down the gangway and joined them. Zircon clapped his hands and instantly a mob was around them. The burly scientist pointed to half a dozen out of the tattered crowd, then indicated their personal baggage, piled on the ship's deck.

The chosen half dozen swarmed to the deck, hoisted the suitcases and trunks to their heads, and came back again, looking expectantly at Zircon.

At once a new crowd gathered, this time made up of men with a more prosperous look to them. Some wore red fezzes on their heads, and one had a felt hat.

"Speech Eengleesh, sar!" the one with the felt hat said.

Zircon nodded to him, and to one of the men wearing a red fez. "Green's Hotel," he bellowed.

They ran off, followed by the porters with the luggage carried on their heads.

Rick and Scotty looked at each other and grinned. Zircon had the situation well in hand.

A little man with a shiny black hat and an equally shiny black frock coat approached, bowing and smiling. He wore tight-fitting white trousers and had no shoes.

Weiss lowered his voice and spoke to the boys. "A Parsee. They're merchants, mostly. Wonder what this one wants?"

The Parsee addressed them all impartially, his eyes going from one to the other. "I am from the hotel," he informed them in excellent English. "You are Dr. Zircon and party?"

"That is correct," Zircon replied.

"I have a truck," the Parsee said. "You have many heavy boxes for the hotel warehouse? I am to take them for you."

Zircon breathed a sigh of relief. "I was wondering how we would get the equipment to the hotel." He pointed to the crates on the schooner's deck. "There it is. Have you men to help you?"

"All is arranged, sir," the Parsee informed him. He waved his hand, and half a dozen men came running. Across the dock, a blunt-nosed truck coughed into life and roared toward them.

Under the Parsee's direction, the equipment was loaded in a few minutes. Then the black-hatted man bowed. "This will be taken to the hotel warehouse."

"Wait," Weiss said nervously. "Hobart, we shouldn't leave the equipment. I'm afraid—" he hesitated.

"You're right, Julius," Zircon agreed.

"I'll go with it," Scotty offered, "and meet you at the hotel. I'd feel better, too, if one of us kept an eye on it."

"Want me to come?" Rick asked.

"No, don't bother. One is enough."

"Okay," Rick said. "Don't get into trouble."

"And see that they're careful of it," Weiss added.

Scotty climbed on the truck and took a seat on top of the equipment. The porters climbed on with him. He waved gaily as the truck turned out through the gate.

Zircon led the way across the pier to where the man in the felt hat and the one in the red fez waited beside old-fashioned, horse-drawn open carriages. "Gharries," the big scientist said. "Not as fast as taxicabs, but a lot safer."

The baggage was stowed in one and the three climbed into the one driven by the man in the felt hat.

Once they left the dock area, there were streetcars, and busses, and even motion-picture theaters. In the center of intersections, little purple- and yellow-clad policemen directed traffic from under huge umbrellas carried on a frame in their belts.

The gharry pulled up before a tall brick structure with a wide balcony just above the street. A uniformed doorman in the inevitable turban ran to meet them, touching his hand to his forehead, lips, and heart in the Moslem fashion. "Salaam, Sahibs," he greeted them. "Welcome to Green's Hotel!"

They registered and were taken to their rooms, which

were sparsely furnished with wicker furniture. Rick unpacked and stowed his clothes, thinking that Scotty should be along soon. When his own stuff was arranged, he unpacked his friend's bag, then went into the professors' room.

"I'm hungry," he announced.

"Youth," Zircon sighed. "It can eat even in heat like this!" He mopped his face with a large handkerchief. "Very well, let us go to the dining room. Scotty can join us there."

They chose a table at the railing of the open-air dining room, and waiters came running with menus. Rick looked around curiously. Most of the diners were Indians, well dressed in Western suits. There was a sprinkling of British uniforms, and a few Europeans in white linens.

"Do you suppose any of this is safe to eat?" Weiss asked.

"Of course," Zircon assured him. "I myself will have the beefsteak."

There was a polite cough and they turned to see a man dressed in immaculate white linen, smiling down at them. He had very short, reddish-brown hair and sharp eyes, and he carried an expensive riding crop. "Your pardon, gentlemen," he said. "I was sitting at the next table and I couldn't help overhearing. I thought I would warn you that the beef is, unfortunately, quite apt to be camel."

"Camel!" Rick exclaimed.

"I'm afraid so. There is a meat shortage in India, you

see, and beef is quite rare. Our Indian friends provide camel, so that the visitors who want beef need not be disappointed."

"It is very kind of you to warn us, sir," Weiss said.

The stranger bowed. "Permit me to introduce myself. I am Hendrick Van Groot. You, of course, are Drs. Zircon and Weiss, and this young man would be . . . is it Scott or Brant?"

"Brant," Rick replied. He noticed a sharp, pungent odor, very familiar, that seemed to hang over Van Groot like an aura. He tried to identify it but couldn't quite remember.

"Won't you join us?" Zircon invited cordially.

"Thank you." Van Groot pulled out the chair next to Rick and sat down. "The *Times of India* carried a complete report on your coming radar experiment, a short time ago. I was very interested because I have traveled Tibet extensively. In fact, I know the Tengi-Bu Plateau quite well."

Rick listened in silence as the scientists exclaimed their delight in meeting someone who knew their destination. He decided Van Groot was a very unusual man. Only someone remarkable would be able to keep his linen suit so immaculate and well pressed in the heat. Rick's own clothes were long since limp and wrinkled.

Van Groot noted a fleck of dust on his spotless sleeve and produced a tissue from an inner pocket. He flicked the tiny bit of dust off, and the odor struck Rick's nostrils again, but stronger.

"Menthol!" he exclaimed.

Van Groot turned to him with a smile. "Yes. I purchase these tissues and place menthol crystals in the box. You see, I have lived in India and the Orient most of my life, and I have learned the value of caution. If one wishes to avoid disease, it is best never to touch things with the bare hands. These disposable tissues are invaluable. The menthol is . . . shall we say a cover-up? My nose dislikes many of the odors of India."

The scientists nodded. "Quite right," Weiss said.

Rick remained silent. He had his own opinions about a man who was so fussy. Besides, he didn't like the odor of menthol. It reminded him of cold medicines. He stirred restlessly. What was keeping Scotty?

"I can recommend the curried lamb," Van Groot said. "They do it very well here."

At Zircon's questioning glance, Rick nodded. Curried lamb was all right with him, whatever it was.

When the waiter had taken their order, Van Groot asked, "Have you chosen your route to the plateau yet? I may be able to help, if you wish."

"The route has been decided by—" Weiss began.

There was a commotion at the door of the dining room. Rick turned to see what the trouble was. As he did, an incredibly dirty little native boy broke loose from the restraining hands of the waiters and ran across the dining room toward them.

The boy dodged the outstretched hands and ran to their table, the waiters in pursuit. "Sahibs!" he gasped. "I have a thing I wish to say!"

Then the waiters were upon him. He struggled, but

they picked him up bodily, smothering his angry yells. In a moment he was out of the room and they heard the clatter as the waiters rushed him down the stairs.

"Now what do you suppose he wanted?" Rick asked, puzzled.

Van Groot shrugged. "Doubtless he had some tale to get money. This is a nation of beggars, you know. They are great hands at inventing tales that will bring a rupee or two."

Zircon spoke up. "What do you suppose is keeping Scotty?"

"He *is* rather late," Weiss said worriedly. "Rick, why don't you go to the lobby? He may be waiting for us at the desk."

Rick rose and, excusing himself, turned to leave, then stopped short with a gasp.

Scotty was just coming into the dining room. His white suit was dusty and stained, and his hair was disheveled. He strode up to the table, rubbing a large purple bruise on his forehead. The boy looked from face to face, his lips pressed tight together.

"The equipment is gone," he announced harshly.

CHAPTER VI

Enter Chahda

For an instant there was silence around the table, then they were all talking at once.

Professor Weiss wrung his hands. "Scotty, are you sure? This is terrible! The equipment can't be gone. Hobart, do you hear? It must be a mistake."

"It's no mistake, sir," Scotty said.

Zircon put a shaking hand on the boy's shoulder. "There must be some explanation, son. Surely the equipment couldn't be stolen in broad daylight."

"I was riding on the back of the truck," Scotty explained. "We went through the gate and into the city, and then one of the natives pushed me from behind. I fell off the truck and cracked my head. It dazed me, I guess, because when I got up the truck was gone."

Weiss slumped into his chair. "I knew it," he groaned. "I've had a premonition of disaster. I told you, Hobart!"

Zircon ignored his distressed colleague. "Go on, son."

"I hailed a taxi and had him take me to the hotel warehouse. It's right around the corner from here. I thought it might have been an accident and the truck would show up. It didn't, so I came over to find you."

Zircon's face was pale, but he was calm. "Are you sure it was the right warehouse?"

"Yes, sir. I checked. Besides, the hotel clerk said they didn't send anyone because they weren't sure when we'd dock."

Van Groot spoke up. "But who on earth would steal your scientific equipment?"

"Conway," Rick muttered bitterly.

Van Groot's eyebrows went up. "Indeed? And who is Conway?"

"I wish we knew," Zircon said shortly. The big man's face was set in a determined expression. "We'll find out, never fear! Well, I suppose our first step is to go to the police."

Julius Weiss had been completely stunned by the news. But now he leaped to his feet and objected shrilly, "No, Hobart! The police are fools! We must go to the American consul and demand men to search. We *must* get the equipment back and at once, do you hear?"

"You are right," Zircon agreed. "It is best for the consul to handle this."

Weiss was paper-white, but he had regained control of himself. "You had better do something about that bruise," he told Scotty. "It must be very painful."

"It is," Scotty answered, then added bitterly, "Let it ache. It will remind me not to be such a dope again."

"Take it easy," Rick said. "It wasn't your fault."

"Of course not," Zircon agreed. "Well, let us go. The sooner we find the consul, the sooner he can get started on the trail of our equipment."

Van Groot dusted an imaginary speck of dust from his trousers with a mentholated tissue. "If I can be of aid, gentlemen, do not hesitate to call upon me," he said suavely. "I am registered here at the hotel."

The party hurried out and walked down the flight of steps to the street level, Rick and Scotty behind the professors.

"Who is that man?" Scotty wanted to know.

Rick explained, then added, "He's a queer duck. I don't like him."

As they went out the front door of the hotel, the beggar boy who had invaded the dining room hurried up, only to be chased away by the doorman.

Gharries were lined up beyond the door. Zircon hailed two, and they got in. The ancient horses trotted off, the boys following the scientists. Rick noted that the beggar boy was running up the street after them. "Wonder what he wants?"

Scotty looked at the little brown figure. "I don't know what he wants, but I know what he needs: a bath." He grinned weakly. Nothing was very funny right now.

As they passed through the heart of the city, Rick looked behind now and then. The beggar boy was still with them, running along about a block behind. Once, as they stopped for traffic, he almost caught up. Then they moved on and he was left behind again.

"Funny he should tag along like that," Rick commented.

They turned down Ballard Road and in a short while drew up before the building that flew the American flag.

As they went into the consulate, the beggar boy came trotting up. He took Zircon's coattail and tugged. "Please, Sahib! You listen?"

Zircon looked down absently. "Go away."

Then they were through the doors and the boy was left outside.

The American consular secretary listened to their story gravely, and made copious notes on his pad. "I'll do what I can," he promised. "It's too late to expect any action today, however." He glanced at his watch. "I'm afraid the police commissioner has been gone for some time, but I'll call his office. They may have a file on Conway. You'll hear from me in the morning."

As the others left, Rick lingered. "Can you change some money for me?"

"Of course." The secretary drew out neat packets of rupee notes and made change for Rick's American money. Rick thanked him and ran to join the others.

Out on the sidewalk, Scotty was waiting alone.

"The professors grabbed a gharry and headed for the Asiatic Geographical Union to talk with the people there. Then they're going to Captain Marks and see if he can help them get any more information out of Meekin."

"I'm afraid it won't do much good," Rick said unhappily. "Hello—here's our friend."

The little beggar boy approached timidly, his brown face split by a white-toothed smile.

"Hello, Sahibs," he greeted them.

"Hello," Rick answered cautiously.

The native boy only came to Rick's shoulder, but on second glance appeared older than he had in the dining room. Rick guessed his age at about fifteen. He was dirty and ragged, but there was something about his face and his cheerful grin that appealed to Rick, and he smiled back.

The boy inspected Rick carefully, then turned his glance to Scotty while they waited good-naturedly to see what he wanted.

"These clothes much good, I think," the native boy said at last. "You buy clothes for me when I tell you a good thing?"

"It depends." Rick grinned. "What is it?"

"You buy me clothes," the native boy said, "and I take you to man which drives the truck with your boxes of stuffs!"

CHAPTER VII

The Man in the Red Turban

"YOU'LL get the new suit," Rick promised. "Now start talking, young fella!"

"My name Chahda," the Hindu boy said. "It means number fo'teen my language. I am fo'teen child in my family."

"What do you know about our equipment?" Scotty asked impatiently.

"I am at dock when the ship comes," Chahda explained. "I see the boxes put on truck, and I see this man who drives, and I know him. He is not a good man, this one. He is a thief.

"I thinks there is dirty works," Chahda continued, "so I chase the truck. I see the Sahib be push off. Soon the truck goes fast-fast, and I not follow. I go to Green's Hotel, but the men do not let me talk with you."

"But you know where this driver lives?"

"Yes," Chahda assented.

"Why did you chase the truck?" Scotty demanded.

The boy shrugged expressively. "I think maybe the 'Merican Sahibs they will give me many rupees."

"You'll get many rupees, all right," Rick promised. "Just lead us to this truck driver."

Chahda hesitated. "It is far, and it is not a good place for Sahibs to go when it is dark."

Rick glanced at the sky. The sun had gone down and dusk was falling rapidly. "Where is this place?"

"You know Crawford Market? Foras Road?"

Rick shook his head. "No. Where are they?"

"Far. Better we go 'morrow."

"We go tonight," Rick insisted. "Or no rupees."

Chahda shrugged. He hailed a gharry and spoke volubly in Hindustani, then he bowed as a signal for the boys to get in. They sat in the back, and Chahda climbed to the little seat at the front and sat facing them. The gharry moved off.

They left the business section of the city and drove down into a quarter where white men were few. This was the crowded Crawford Market section, the native markets that housed the shops of the silversmiths, the coppersmiths, the vendors of birds and monkeys and wicked-looking knives, and strange foodstuffs and exotic fabrics.

As they progressed deeper into the quarter, the number of people seemed to increase. Men and boys ran alongside the carriage, holding up their wares, or shouting "Alms, for the love of Allah!"

Chahda called out to them in a curt manner, then

explained to the boys, "I tell them go away, or maybe I call the cops."

Rick and Scotty grinned at his use of American slang. Chahda was an amazing little fellow. They were further amazed, when Rick exclaimed at the numbers of people, for the Hindu boy announced:

"This population Bombay, he is one million four hun'red thousan'. Same like Conn-eck-tee-kut in 'Merica."

He continued with studied nonchalance, just as though the two white boys were not staring at him popeyed.

"Maybeso these Conn-eck-tee-kut have more peoples now. When they count noses in nineteen-twenty, it has one million three hun'red eighty thousan', almost like Bombay, I think."

Rick's jaw was hanging slack. "Did you get that, Scotty? The population of Connecticut, according to the 1920 census! Chahda, where did you get that information?"

Chahda looked pleased. "Oh, I know many things about this 'Merica. I have readed a book."

"I believe it," Scotty said. "Where did you learn English?"

"For many years, maybe two, maybe three, I am houseboy for a missionary man in Nepal. He is teach me. I speak good, yes?"

"Yes," Rick agreed. "What book did you read?"

Chahda smiled comfortably. "It is a very val . . . val . . ."

"Valuable?"

"Yes. My father has it for a long time. He is find it when a train is wreck. Some things I do not understan', but the missionary he is help me. I read some more, and I remember all these things."

"But what was this book?"

Chahda said proudly, "It is call 'The Worrold Alm-in-ack.'"

"*The World Almanac!*" Rick choked back a laugh, not wanting to hurt Chahda's feelings. He had a vision of the boy sitting by the hour, memorizing the facts in the *Almanac.*

"Why did you try to remember the facts, Chahda?" he asked.

"Someday I will go to 'Merica," the Hindu boy answered. "It will be so good to know these thing. Yes?"

"Yes," Rick agreed. There seemed to be no other answer.

The gharry rolled on through the market district into a quarter where the houses were of flimsy wooden construction, and close together. It was a place of dim light and foul odors, and misery beyond anything Rick had ever imagined. Chahda had certainly brought them to the worst quarter of Bombay.

"I think I know now why Van Groot carries menthol in his pocket," Rick commented wryly.

"Check," Scotty said. "Rick, I don't like this part of town. Notice the way the people look at us?"

"We go back?" Chahda asked hopefully.

"No. We're here; we mav as well see about this truck

driver." Rick didn't like the looks of the quarter, either, but he was determined to find the driver who had gone off with the equipment.

Chahda called up to their driver and the gharry stopped. "We here," the native boy told them.

They paid the gharry driver, then Chahda led the way up a dismal-looking alley and stopped before a crude door. "More better we not go in," he said.

"Let's go," Rick answered quietly, though he was feeling far from calm. Anything could happen in this part of town.

Chahda pushed open the door.

They went into a low-ceilinged room in which many tables were set. The foul air made Rick choke. Guttering candles were the only illumination. They cast a wavering light on the face of the sole occupant, who was seated at one of the tables, his head bowed over a cup.

As they entered, he looked up and Scotty clutched Rick's arm. The pock-marked face and the red turban were those of the truck driver!

"Chahda," Rick said tensely, "ask him where he took the stuff?"

Chahda spouted voluble syllables.

The driver looked up warily, then deliberately swung his chair around and turned his back on them.

"He no talk. We go, yes?" Chahda urged.

A door in the back of the room opened and a second man came in. He had a pointed face, half hidden by a sloppily tied turban. Scotty recognized him.

Rick heard his friend's voice rise angrily. "That's the one who pushed me off the truck!"

He saw the newcomer and the truck driver reach into the folds of their clothes, saw the flicker of candlelight on gleaming steel, and he saw Scotty jump forward!

With a yell, he grabbed Scotty's right arm and held on while Chahda leaped forward and grabbed the other arm. Together they rushed him out into the alley.

CHAPTER VIII

The Fight in the Warehouse

"WHAT did you do that for?" Scotty demanded furiously.

"They had knives," Rick explained. He held on to Scotty's arm. "Getting yourself cut up wouldn't solve anything."

"They use knives," Chahda supplied. "They kill quick, those men. I know!"

"Let's get out of here," Rick said. "We can find a cop and bring him back."

Scotty followed as he led the way out of the alley. The ex-marine was grumbling, but he realized the senselessness of getting into a brawl.

Far down the road they found one of the youthful-looking policemen. He listened to Chahda's story, then went back with them. He took a firm grip on his club and pushed open the door, Rick and Scotty crowding in after him.

The room was empty.

"Back here," Scotty said, and made his way through

the tables to the door through which the second man had entered.

"It's no use, Scotty. They're gone," Rick said.

The policeman shrugged. Chahda interpreted. "He is sorry, but if them men are gone, there is no thing he can do."

"I guess not," Rick agreed. "Thank him anyway, Chahda."

The policeman bowed and went back to his post. Rick looked helplessly at Scotty and Chahda. "What do we do now?"

"Nothing," Scotty replied gloomily. "We can go back to the hotel and tell the professors what happened. They can notify the consul in the morning. Maybe Chahda can lead a police squad back again, but I don't think they'll find anything."

Outside the alley, it was almost fully night. Here and there street lights penetrated the falling gloom, but most places were dark. Rick looked around for a gharry, but there was none in sight. Their own driver, foolishly had been paid and told to go. Gharries didn't haunt this section where no one had money enough for fare.

"We may as well walk back," he suggested.

Chahda spoke up. "It is not far. And we walk in middle of street, yes? Then no one jump from doorways with knife."

"A nice, cheerful little kid," Scotty remarked. "How old are you, Chahda?"

"Maybe fifteen, maybe sixteen. Not know for sure."

"That's pretty young to know so much about thieving truck drivers," Rick said jokingly.

Chahda considered. "Maybe so. But same in India as in 'Merica. Most peoples is young before they grow up."

"That's the wisdom of the Orient we've heard about." Scotty grinned.

"In 'Merica, when count noses in 1920, is thirt'-three million six hun'red thousan's little kids under fo'teen years age. That is what says the Alm-in-ack," Chahda announced.

Both boys burst out laughing.

"You're going to be handy to have around," Scotty laughed. "You know more about America than we do."

"This one is a smart cookie," Chahda agreed, showing his white teeth in a pleased grin.

They had reached Crawford Market again. Here, in the narrow, shop-lined streets, vendors plied their wares. Torches flared, augmenting the feeble glow of the few electric lights. The flickering light, the dust-choked air, and the teeming, turbaned or fezzed mob in their gay rags reminded Rick once more of a scene from the *Arabian Nights.*

"Look at the crowd over there," Scotty said. "Buying food, I guess."

Rick looked where his friend pointed and saw a dozen men haranguing an elderly man in a black fez behind a stand. There was much waving of hands and much loud language as they bartered. He grinned at the scene, so different from any that might be found in

America. Then the grin froze. Beyond the vendor's stand a man was standing in a doorway . . . a man in a shiny black hat and a shiny frock coat. He wore tight white trousers, and his feet were bare.

The man turned and Rick got a good look at his face. He clutched Scotty's arm. "Over there in the doorway!" Rick whispered. "The Parsee who took our equipment!"

Scotty's eyes sought the doorway. "You're right!" He started to push his way through the crowd.

"Easy," Rick pleaded. "Don't let him see you."

Too late! The Parsee stopped in the act of wiping his face and stared right at them, then he melted into the crowd.

"He saw us," Rick groaned. "We can't follow him in this mob."

Chahda tugged at his sleeve. "If I follow, you give me job?"

"Yes," Rick agreed. "Yes, but hurry, will you?"

"Wait at hotel," Chahda instructed, and was gone into the throng.

"There's a lad who's right on the ball. He waits until he gets you into a corner, then he holds you up," Scotty remarked.

"I guess it's natural," Rick said. "He's never had anything, so when he sees a chance to get ahead, he grabs at it in the only way he knows."

"He's a likable little cuss," Scotty commented. "Isn't it funny the way he pops up with all that strange dope out of *The World Almanac*?"

"It is," Rick agreed, "but it's kind of touching, too. Imagine living in a land where the only book you can get is a copy of *The World Almanac!*"

They passed out of Carnac Road into Mahatma Ghandi Road, and found a gharry at the curb. In a few moments they were rolling down the wide streets of modern Bombay to the hotel.

As they entered the creaky elevator, Scotty asked, "Do you think we ought to tell the professors?"

Rick thought it over, then shook his head. "They're upset enough. No point in getting them excited until we have something definite to report."

There was no light on in the professors' room, but as they tiptoed past, the door opened and Zircon came out.

"Oh, there you are, boys," he said. He looked and sounded tired, his big shoulders slumping. "Julius and I went to the Geographical Union. They were most sympathetic, but there was nothing they could do. Then we went to the jail with Captain Marks and tried to get Meekin to talk."

He rubbed his forehead as though his head ached painfully. "Poor Julius became quite hysterical. I think he would have tried to beat information out of Meekin if I hadn't restrained him. It's obvious the man knows nothing of value. I finally brought Julius home and gave him a sedative. He's sleeping quietly now."

"You'd better get some sleep yourself, sir," Rick urged. "You look tired out."

"I am," Zircon admitted. "But I find it hard to sleep. So much depends on recovering the equipment. So much . . ." his voice trailed off and he nodded a good night, then went back into his room.

Rick looked at Scotty, his eyes troubled. "Let's wash up, and then go down and keep watch for Chahda. It looks like he's our only hope."

"Right," Scotty agreed. "I have a hunch he'll come through for us. I like that little guy. He's right on his toes."

Later, as they walked down by the sea wall, Rick said thoughtfully, "One thing is sure. Whoever is behind all this doesn't want the equipment. Otherwise, Meekin wouldn't have tried to destroy it."

"What does that add up to?" Scotty wanted to know.

"Conway, whoever he is, is trying to stop the experiment."

"That's reasonable," Scotty admitted. "But why?"

"If I could figure that out," Rick said wearily, "I'd tell Sherlock Holmes to move over and I'd set up in the detective business."

They had walked in a circle and were back at the hotel.

"Want to go upstairs and rest?" Rick asked. "The clerk could call us if Chahda should come."

"Too hot," Scotty objected. "I wish there were some way we could sleep out of doors."

"There is," Rick said. He walked across the street to where half a dozen gharries were parked by the curb, drivers and horses nodding sleepily. He hailed the nearest one.

"How much for all night?"

The driver woke up and considered. "Twenty rupees."

"I'll give you five."

"Allah! The Sahib would rob a poor man. No less than eighteen."

"Eight rupees."

"*Bismallah!* Fifteen."

The bargaining closed at eleven rupees and Rick grinned in satisfaction. Haggling over prices was a lot of fun. He directed the gharry to the door of the hotel, then he and Scotty climbed in and made themselves comfortable.

The driver looked at his passengers, scratched his head, shrugged, and was asleep almost at once.

"Why don't you take a cat nap, Rick," Scotty suggested. "We'll have to take turns staying awake in case Chahda should come."

Rick wasn't sure he could sleep but he leaned back against the cushion and in a moment his head dropped.

Suddenly he jerked upright. Scotty was shaking him. "Snap out of it, Rick," Scotty said. "Here's Chahda."

"Huh?" Rick rubbed his eyes. "I must have dozed off."

"And how!" Scotty exclaimed. He swung to the ground. "It's half past four."

Chahda was standing nervously, first on one foot then on the other. "I have found it," he kept saying. "You tell the professor-Sahibs, yes?" he asked Rick.

"I don't know about that. What do you think, Scotty?"

"We'd better not. You know how upset they are. We'd better see if the equipment is really there."

"Right." He motioned Chahda into the gharry. Scotty got back in and sat beside him.

"Tell the driver where to go," Rick said.

Chahda gave brief instructions in his own language, and the tired, bony horse stirred into reluctant life.

They drove through the center of the darkened city, the clop-clop of the hoofs and the creak of the wheels a background for Chahda's tale. He had followed the Parsee to a public eating place, and he had waited while the man ate his supper.

"He ate so much! Then he goes, and I follow. He walks far—oh, very far! He goes down near the Alexandria dock, and then he goes into a place where there is drinks for drinking, and he sits by a table for so long. But I am waiting. He goes down many streets and in many places where I am afraid, but I stay close. Soon he is coming to a big building, and I am looking in."

Chahda paused dramatically. "There is the many box which is been on the truck!"

The gharry had left the center of the city and was now traveling through winding streets that led to the water front. As they neared a street corner, Chahda called to the driver to let them out.

They left the gharry and made their way down a series of narrow lanes edged with dark, forbidding shacks. The water was somewhere near; they heard the mournful wail of a boat whistle, and the sound tightened the short hairs on Rick's scalp.

Chahda was a noiseless wraith scuttling along through

the alleys, but Rick stumbled through debris and into obstacles that bruised his shins. Scotty made no noise except for the sound of his leather soles on the cobbles.

The Hindu boy stopped. "We 'most there," he whispered. "This goes back way, so men not see."

"What men?"

"I think maybe guards. There is fi'-six men."

"Fine," Rick said hoarsely. "Just two to one, that's all."

"We not fight; we look," Chahda assured him.

"Let's keep going," Scotty urged. "I'm anxious to see this place."

There was the sound of water lapping against piers near by, and it was very dark. Rick looked up at the sky through the narrow canyon of wooden buildings and saw that the stars were dimming. Dawn wasn't far away.

A high building loomed, and Chahda put out a hand to stop them. He led them to a window and said, "You look."

Rick looked through a dirt-smeared pane into a barnlike warehouse. Far in the front were lights, against which crates of goods were silhouetted. Against the lights, men moved, turbaned men, with dark, shapeless robes. Then, as his vision adjusted, he saw a thing that he recognized: the antenna base in its open crate, silhouetted against the light!

He gripped Scotty's shoulder. "It's there! Scotty, I saw the antenna base."

"Good. Now what do we do?"

"Get the police," Rick decided. "We can't handle this

alone. I saw at least six men. Chahda, get some policemen, and hurry! We'll stay here and wait for you." He added, "I'm not going to take my eyes off that equipment again!"

Chahda vanished into the dimness.

"Let's work around toward the front," Scotty whispered. "I'd like to get a better look."

"So would I," Rick answered.

They groped their way around a corner of the building and came out in another alley. Toward the front there were other windows through which faint light streamed.

Rick pressed close to the wall and edged his way toward the nearest window. They were close to the front now and the voices of the guards were audible. He was breathing hard through tight lips. If they were discovered before help came, it might go hard with them. The truck driver had been an example of the kind of people they were dealing with.

He peered into the window, Scotty looking over his shoulder. A huge crate blocked the view. He stepped back. "Not there. Maybe the next one."

Scotty nodded and motioned for him to continue.

Rick, his eyes on the next window, stepped forward —and his foot sank into something that gave under him.

There was an ear-piercing scream from under his feet, and he jumped back and fell against Scotty. They went down in a heap as a sheeted figure scrambled to its feet and ran down the alley, filling the night with cries of terror. Rick had stepped on a sleeping Indian.

Scotty scrambled to his feet. "Are you hurt?" he asked hoarsely.

"No," Rick said. "I'm . . ." His eyes caught movement toward the front of the building, and he yelled, "Scotty, watch out!"

He jumped to his feet as his friend whirled to meet the rush of guards. He saw Scotty's hand lash out, held stiff in a judo blow, and he saw a robed figure go down. Then three of them were almost upon him.

Rick side-stepped the rush and lifted his foot as though punting a football. It connected with something soft, and a cry of pain split the air. He jumped back and caught a glimpse of something flying toward him, blotting out the faint light, then he was wrapped in the smothering folds of harsh, foul cloth. Something hit him below the ribs and he went over on his back, stunned.

He felt himself lifted, and heard other cries, and knew that Scotty wasn't down yet. He tried to lash out with his feet, but numbness gripped him and his breath came in short, painful gasps. Then there was only silence and the swaying of the shoulders under him as he was carried into the warehouse.

Many minutes passed before he came back to full consciousness, gasping for air in the folds of the cloth that bound him. He heard voices, but they were not speaking English. Then he was put down on something hard and the cloth was whisked away.

He blinked up into the flame of a single candle and knew he was on the floor in some part of the warehouse.

Men looked down at him—men with turbans, and coarse dark faces. He struggled to a sitting position and saw Scotty next to him, flat on his back, his eyes closed.

Rick tried to get to his feet, but one of the men pushed him back. He saw the gleam of light on a blade as the man drew a curved, scimitarlike knife from the folds of his robe. He swallowed hard.

The man lifted the knife and waved it expressively. Rick tried to take his eyes from the gleaming blade but could not.

There was a chair next to the boy, a wooden kitchen chair, sagging with age. The man lifted the knife again, and this time brought it down sharply. The keen edge sliced through the back of the chair as though the slab of wood didn't exist. It didn't even make a crunching noise.

The man grinned and waved the knife again. He went out, taking the candle. The others went with him. The door closed and a key grated in the lock.

Instantly Rick was at Scotty's side. He put a hand on the boy's heart and found it beating strongly. He gave a sigh of relief and started probing for wounds. There were none. Then, just above the bruise on Scotty's forehead, he found a lump. As he touched it, Scotty groaned and moved.

"Scotty!" Rick whispered. "Wake up, Scotty." He shook him a little.

After a few moments Scotty sat up and put both hands to his head. "Rick, are you all right?"

"I'm okay. What happened to you?"

"One of them hit me with the flat of his knife. I thought I was dead."

"If they'd hit you with the edge . . ." Rick gulped, and told Scotty about the chair. "That was to show me what would happen if we tried to get out."

"I'm convinced," Scotty said.

They inspected their prison and found it to be a small, square room, unfurnished except for the broken chair. Then Rick found a crack through which faint light streamed. He put his eye to it and looked out into the warehouse.

They were at the top of a flight of stairs. Below them was the big floor of the warehouse with its stacked crates and bales. Not all of this stuff was theirs, but some of it was. Rick could see the wide entrance doors, the guards squatting by it. He counted five men. Hadn't there been more than that? Perhaps some had left.

"Maybe they sent word to the boss that they captured us," Rick guessed.

"Yes, but who is this boss?"

"Conway," Rick replied. It was the only answer they had.

There was a stir at the front of the building, and the guards got to their feet and began talking in low tones.

"Something's happening," Rick said.

Chahda came through the main entrance with two policemen!

"He came back with the police," Rick added joyfully. Scotty crowded close so that he could see through the crack.

At the front of the building, the guards, the police, and Chahda were engaged in loud conversation in Hindustani, with much waving of arms.

"Why don't the cops arrest them?" Scotty demanded.

"It's only Chahda's word against the guards'," Rick replied. "Listen, we have to get out of here! Those guys will convince the cops nothing is wrong!"

Scotty examined the door. "Not very strong. Maybe . . ."

"Let's try it," Rick urged.

They backed across the room and put their shoulders down.

"Now!" Rick yelled.

They smashed into the door. It groaned on its hinges but didn't give.

"Again!"

They hit it with the force of desperation. The door flew open with a crashing of panels, and they were catapulted onto the stair landing in a heap.

There were excited yells from below. Rick and Scotty scrambled to their feet and saw the flash of knives!

As they ran to the aid of the police, Rick saw one of the policemen dance away from a knife thrust. His wooden club flicked out and caught his opponent over the eyes. The man crumpled to the floor. Then, so quickly that he was a blur, the little policeman stepped in and swung again, and a second of the guards went down.

But fast as the Bombay police were, they were outnumbered. Scotty went into the fight in a headlong rush.

Rick gasped in horror as he saw a wicked blade lifted high over his friend's head. He grabbed at a loose board and flung it with all his strength. The board whirled through the air, caught the knife wielder's uplifted arm, and caromed into a second man. Then Scotty swung from the hip and the man with the knife crashed against the wall.

Rick jumped for the board and lifted it, swinging it like a flail. Once a knife thrust dug splinters from his weapon, and he brought it down on the head of his opponent. The board cracked and the man rocked, but his turban saved him. He lifted his knife and jumped for Rick. A brown leg was thrust out and Chahda kicked the man's feet from under him.

Then it was all over. One of the little officers stepped behind Rick's opponent and did something with his hands. When he stepped away, the man's wrists were neatly tied behind him. The other policeman was busy, too, with short lengths of rope. In a few minutes all five of the guards were trussed up.

In another ten minutes the warehouse was cleared of men except for Rick, Scotty, Chahda, and one officer. Their prisoners had been taken away in a police wagon that had appeared promptly. The lack of formality amazed the boys. They promised to appear with the American consul to press charges, and that was that. An officer was placed on duty, in case the missing guards showed up.

"Holy smoke! I never saw anything happen so fast," Scotty declared.

Rick was already busy checking over the crates of equipment. "It's all here," he announced at last. "Now what do we do?"

"Call the professors and have them get a truck," Scotty suggested.

"Wait a minute . . . I have an idea." Rick turned to Chahda. "Can you get a dozen gharries?"

"Can do," Chahda promised. He left at a run.

"We'll pile it in gharries and take it back to the hotel," Rick said. "Won't the professors be surprised?"

"They'll be flabbergasted," Scotty agreed, grinning. "I am, myself."

Outside, it was almost full dawn. They went to the door of the warehouse and looked past low sheds across the water. It was cool now, and the dawn breeze was fragrant.

"I'm beginning to like India," Rick remarked. He was so relieved at having the equipment back that he could have done a war dance.

There was a great rattle of wheels and pounding of hoofs as Chahda appeared with a procession of gharries. The Hindu boy sat up on the high seat next to the leading gharry driver, his arms folded and his head as high as that of any conquering hero.

The dozen gharry drivers clustered around and there was much talk in broken English and Hindustani before Chahda finally conveyed the idea. Then they boggled at the idea of doing manual labor, like lifting boxes. This, they proclaimed with outraged dignity, was beneath them.

Rick waved rupees and the drivers reconsidered. Maybe it wasn't so far beneath their dignity after all. How many rupees extra did the Sahib say?

At last, with great tumult and excitement, the equipment was loaded into the dozen open carriages.

Rick, flushed with victory, climbed to the driver's seat of the leading gharry. Scotty and Chahda rode in back, like princes of royal blood, as Rick and his laughing but slightly bewildered driver led the procession through the awakening, dawnlit streets of Bombay to the hotel.

CHAPTER IX

Chahda Disappears

The gharries drew up outside the hotel with a great confusion of neighing horses and shouting drivers. The doorman took one look and ran, appearing in a moment with the sleepy clerk.

Rick assured the clerk that it was not an invasion, then joined Scotty and Chahda. "Now that we're here, where do we take the stuff?"

"The warehouse," Scotty suggested.

"I hate to let it out of our sight," Rick said. "How about taking it into the hotel?"

"Sure. Then we can keep an eye on it."

The idea was translated into action. To the night clerk's horror, the gharry drivers fell to with a will and toted the crates into the hotel, piling them squarely in the middle of the lobby.

Rick, who had been outside pleading with the drivers not to drop anything, went into the hotel and stopped short at the sight of the equipment piled in the middle of the floor.

"Good night!" he exclaimed. "I didn't mean them to pile it right in the middle of the lobby!"

"Why not?" Scotty demanded. "I'd like to see anyone steal it from there."

The night clerk had both hands on his head and was shaking it, calling upon the sacred names of his Hindu gods to give him strength and wisdom that he might know how to deal with these insane Sahibs. Despairing, he ran for the manager.

Rick, Scotty, and Chahda went out to pay off their gharry drivers. There was the usual haggling, with Chahda taking part, then Rick added an extra five-rupee note for each.

"Now," he said, "I'm broke."

"I still have a little money," Scotty said.

"Come on, we have to tell the professors about this."

As Rick turned to go into the hotel, the manager and the clerk burst through the door, followed by Zircon and Weiss.

The professors rushed up to the boys and anxiously asked if they were all right. Assured that they were, the scientists went to check their precious equipment.

Julius Weiss counted aloud. Then, satisfied that the crates were all there, he turned to the boys with almost tearful relief. "Now," he said, "we want to hear all about it. Let's get Hobart and we'll go to your room."

Hobart Zircon's voice rose as he argued with the irate manager, but on the professor's promise that the equipment would be moved very shortly, he quieted down and serenity reigned in the lobby once more.

It was breakfast time before their story was told. The scientists sat on Rick's bed and listened with open mouths. When the boys finished, the scientists exclaimed in unison, "What would your father say if he knew we had let you get into a mess like that?"

The boys had been changing their clothes and getting cleaned up, as they talked. Chahda sat on the floor, his face one big smile.

"We have to get Chahda a suit," Rick said. "And we have to hire him. We promised."

"A promise it's a pleasure to keep," Zircon declared. He produced some rupees from his wallet and handed them to Chahda. "Here, my lad. Go do your shopping and get cleaned up. We'll talk about that job when you come back."

Chahda bowed three times, turned and bumped into the door jamb, bowed again, and fled down the hall toward the stairs.

Scotty grinned. "That new suit means a lot to him. And he certainly earned it."

"Now," Julius Weiss suggested, in high spirits, "let us repair to breakfast, gentlemen. I must admit this excitement has given me an appetite. I fear neither Hobart nor I have eaten since the equipment was lost."

Over breakfast they held a council of war.

"I see no reason why we can't leave today," Zircon said. "There are a number of things we must do, however. Julius, will you see about getting the replacement parts, also the extra provisions and medicines we will need? The company will expect you, so there should be no delay."

Weiss nodded.

"I will take care of our travel arrangements. Fortunately it was all arranged by mail, so only a few details need to be cleared up."

Rick spoke up. "Scotty and I have to go with the American consul to the police, to identify those men and press charges."

"Hmmm." Zircon was thoughtful. "That may take some time. I had hoped . . ."

A familiar voice, accompanied by the scent of menthol, interrupted. "Good morning, gentlemen. May I congratulate you on your good fortune?"

Hendrick Van Groot stood smiling at them, immaculate as ever in freshly starched whites, a mentholated tissue in his hand.

The professors greeted him cordially and invited him to sit down. He beamed at Rick and Scotty. "That was quite an adventure these young men had. The manager told me about it." He turned to Zircon. "Now you can continue your trip, eh?"

"We plan to leave today, if we can complete the arrangements."

"If I can be of any assistance, please call upon me."

Zircon's brows furrowed. "Perhaps you can, sir. I was just about to say, when you arrived, that Julius and I went to the Asiatic Geographical Union last night to see about our maps . . ."

"We met several of our Indian colleagues," Weiss

said. "Most interesting. But we were too late, and the vaults were locked. So we must get the maps this morning."

"Perhaps I could pick them up for you? I know the people at the Union very well. In fact, they have prepared maps for me several times."

"That would be most kind," Zircon said.

Van Groot reached into an inner pocket and produced a pen and notebook. "Perhaps you had better write a note giving them permission to turn the maps over to me."

"Of course." Zircon scrawled the note and signed it. "Now, I think everything is arranged. Thanks to Hartson Brant's foresight, we have little to do." Then he added grimly, "I feel that we will be much safer on the trail."

As Van Groot departed, Julius Weiss said, "It was most kind of him to offer to get the maps. I'm sure he's thoroughly reliable. We have a number of mutual acquaintances, he tells me, and he is a member of the Netherlands Academy of Science."

The morning passed in a fever of activity. Rick and Scotty went to the police court, accompanied by the obliging consular secretary. The warehouse guards were brought in, identified, and charged. But none of them would talk. To all questions they presented a stolid, silent front. Nor would they admit knowing Conway. There was nothing in the police files of a confidence man by that name.

Rick left the station with a feeling of frustration. "We

don't know any more than we did before," he complained. Then he gave a little shudder. "When I saw those guards in the daylight, it scared me to death. I never saw a tougher-looking bunch."

"It gave me a queer feeling, too," Scotty admitted. "We're lucky we didn't get our throats cut."

Back at the hotel, Professor Zircon was waiting. He had made arrangements for train compartments and travel permissions without difficulty. The train was to leave at two o'clock. It was already after eleven.

Julius Weiss returned. The provisions and equipment were to be delivered to the train. There had been no difficulty; he had been expected.

Then Chahda appeared. He came to the door, smiled and bowed, and they bowed back, not recognizing him at once.

"This Chahda," he said. "You forget?"

Rick let out a whoop while the others stared in amazement.

Chahda was dressed in spotless white linen with a white shirt and a bright yellow tie. On his formerly bare feet were white shoes and yellow socks. He was scrubbed until his brown face gleamed, and on his head was a turban of white with yellow threads. He looked more like the son of some fabled maharajah than the beggar boy with *The World Almanac* education.

As Rick, Scotty, and the professors shook hands with him solemnly, he almost burst with pride.

"Now," he announced, "I be your Number One boy."

In the midst of packing, Van Groot arrived with a

map case under his arm. They gathered around him in the professors' room, Chahda peering inquisitively past Rick's arm.

"Sorry I took so long," Van Groot apologized. He wiped his face with a mentholated tissue. "The man in charge of the vaults had gone off on an errand and I had to wait until he returned."

"Let us look at them," Weiss suggested eagerly.

Zircon took the case and thumbed through several maps. "This is the important one," he said, "the section from the last Tibetan town to the plateau."

He unfolded the map and spread it on the bed. Instantly six heads were bent over it.

"Ah," Van Groot said, "they have chosen the very best route for you. I know it well. The other trails are almost impassable for yaks and donkeys."

"I don't see Mount Everest," Scotty commented.

"It's not on here. Our trail takes us well away from Everest," Zircon answered. "We may not even see it."

Chahda tugged at Rick's sleeve and motioned with his head toward the next room. Rick followed, curious, and Scotty joined them as the professors and Van Groot launched into a discussion of the route.

In the boys' room, Chahda said: "When I am in Nepal, I hear much from Sahibs who are making climbs to Tibet. And always they are making talks about places not on those maps."

"What do you mean, Chahda?" Rick asked.

"The path is not how these Sahibs in Nepal say they go to Tengi-Bu."

Rick and Scotty exchanged glances.

"Perhaps not," Rick replied. "But there must be more than one way to get to the plateau. The Asiatic Geographical people just picked one you hadn't heard of."

"Sure," Scotty agreed.

"Not think so," Chahda insisted stubbornly. "Path on maps is maybe wrong way."

"But you don't know that it is," Scotty objected.

"This one knows," Chahda replied with dignity.

Rick saw that further argument would hurt the boy's feelings. "Well, maybe you're right, Chahda. But I don't think Professor Zircon would want to change the route without proof."

He was saved from further discussion by a loud knocking on the door.

The manager stood there, and he was wringing his hands. "Please, Sahibs," he wailed. "You come, yes? Those gharry drivers! They are making ruin of my hotel. You come?"

"Right away," Rick said. He started to ask what drivers, but the distraught manager ran ahead, down to the lobby. All seemed quiet there, barring the presence of crates in the center of the floor.

"Outside," the manager said. "You will see."

The boys hurried to the front entrance and stopped short at a sight that made it difficult to keep a poker face.

The gharry drivers had taken up quarters in front of the hotel. Rick's large tip had seemed to them a promise of more rupees from the generous Sahibs. Their families had joined them. One group was cooking a meal over a fire in a charcoal brazier right in front of the door. Little children were running around happily. Some of the drivers were asleep.

Scotty pointed, and Rick looked over to where one of them was being shaved by a barber called in for the occasion. There were so many that they blocked traffic, and the din was appalling.

The professors and Van Groot appeared and looked out at the confusion in the street. Zircon came to the manager's rescue with an order to the drivers to load the equipment at once.

In a few moments order was restored, the equipment was piled in the gharries, and their personal baggage was brought down. Then, at a word from Zircon, the party piled into the carriages and started for Victoria Railroad Terminus.

Rick looked around at the nearest gharries and asked, "Where's Chahda?"

"In one of the other carriages, I guess," Scotty answered.

"Must be," Rick said, and settled back to enjoy the ride.

But at the railroad station Chahda did not appear. The equipment was loaded into the spare compartment and one of the station guards was detailed to watch it. The gharry drivers were paid off with the usual confusion, then the party took stock.

"That seems to be everything," Zircon said.

"Chahda's missing," Rick reminded him.

"I daresay he'll show up," Van Groot said. "Perhaps

he had some unfinished business." He smiled. "The little beggar seems to be a man of affairs, don't you think?"

Rick didn't like the patronizing tone. "I don't think he'd have gone off without saying something."

"He likely missed us at the hotel," Zircon suggested. "Or he may have gone off for something to eat. I'm sure he'll show up."

"We ourselves had better eat," Weiss said. "You know these Indian trains. It will be several days before we get a decent meal again."

"You shall be my guests," Van Groot announced. He waved the ever-present mentholated tissue. "Now, gentlemen, no refusals! We will have lunch at the Coffee Club on Churchgate Street."

He hailed a taxi and the party climbed in. Rick kept watch for Chahda as they drove down Hornby Road toward Churchgate, but there was no sign of the boy.

"He'll be waiting for us at the train," Scotty said. "He wouldn't take a chance on being left behind."

Van Groot was an excellent and interesting host. He told them tales of the Tibetan country and of the people. "They're Buddhists," he said, "and most faithful to their beliefs. Can't even swat a fly, because harming anything, even a centipede, means loss of merit in the next world. Quite touching, after a fashion."

And he told them tales of Lhasa, the forbidden city of the Dalai Lama, where, unfortunately, their travels would not take them. Before any of them realized it, their time was up and they had to hurry back.

The taxi pulled up at the barnlike railroad station

just as the warning whistle blew. Rick looked around for Chahda. He ran to the nearest official and asked if anyone had inquired for the American party, but the man didn't understand English.

"Hurry, Rick," Zircon called.

The shrill whistle gave a long blast. Rick ran for his compartment, past the second- and third-class carriages, past bearded passengers, hooded Moslem women, ragged Hindus and uniformed colonials, and past goats that traveled with their owners, and chickens in crates, and water carriers with goatskins.

There was no sign of an erect Hindu boy in a new white suit.

Rick climbed into the compartment and said desperately, "He's not here!"

Van Groot stood on the platform, holding a tissue to his nose to guard him from the dust of the station. "Don't imagine that you'll see him again," he remarked. "These little street boys are like that. Most undependable. Well, *bon voyage*. Best of fortune and all that."

The train jerked and began to move. Van Groot lifted the riding crop he carried, in a gesture of farewell. Zircon leaned over and closed the compartment door.

Rick started to protest, but realized the uselessness of it. They couldn't wait for Chahda. He went to the door and looked back along the platform, seeing the figure of Van Groot slowly recede.

Suddenly there was a smaller figure in white running along the platform.

Chahda!

He was running for all he was worth, and he was shouting something Rick couldn't hear.

"Stop the train! Chahda's here!" Rick yelled.

The little figure in white came even with Van Groot, and started to pass him.

Rick saw Van Groot's riding crop go up, then lash down. Chahda's running legs faltered and he fell face down on the platform.

CHAPTER X

The Odor of Menthol

Rick grabbed for the compartment-door handle and started to swing it open, but Scotty caught his arm.

"The train's moving, dope!"

Rick whirled. "Chahda! He's out there. Van Groot knocked him down!"

Scotty pulled him away from the door. "You can't do anything about it now. You'd be killed if you tried to get off!"

"We have to stop the train," Rick said desperately.

The professors joined Scotty.

"It's unfortunate," Zircon spoke with finality. "But there is nothing we can do, Rick. The boy just missed the train, that's all."

"But why did Van Groot hit him?"

"Are you sure he did, Rick?" Weiss asked.

"Of course I'm sure! He was running up the platform, shouting something. When he got to Van Groot, I saw him knock Chahda down with that riding crop he carries."

"Odd," Zircon frowned.

"Maybe he brushed against Van Groot," Scotty suggested. "He doesn't like Indians. He might knock him down."

"That's it, of course," Weiss agreed.

Rick sank into the compartment seat. They were far out of the station now, and railroad yards were giving way to open country. They had crossed the bridge from Bombay to the mainland of India.

"I wonder why Chahda was late?" Rick said, and his thoughts kept going back to the Hindu boy's comments on the map. "He said the route to Tengi-Bu was wrong."

"I imagine the Asiatic Geographical Union knows more about that than Chahda," Weiss remarked.

"Maybe he went to say good-bye to his family," Scotty said.

Zircon shrugged. "Whatever the reason, he's far behind us now. It's regrettable that Van Groot struck him, but I think Scotty's explanation accounts for that. Chahda brushed against him and Van Groot retaliated."

Rick stared morosely out the window. He wasn't satisfied with any of the explanations offered, but he had no better ones to present. They would probably never know, because in a few days Chahda would be a thousand miles behind.

He looked around the compartment, noticing that Zircon had arranged for boxes of rations and for sheets and pillowcases. Their equipment was in the next compartment, the door securely locked. He reached up and turned on the fan and unhappily settled himself for the trip.

Days and nights intermingled and Rick couldn't have said how long they had been traveling. The stops were the only things that broke the monotony. They would get out and walk on the platform to stretch their legs, and crowds of natives would gather at a little distance and watch them.

The crowds were as much a part of India as the clay dust and the red-brass sun. They waited for the train at one stop and the same crowd seemed to be waiting for it at the next, so uniform were they in character. They looked alike, they sounded alike. Their wild cries as they hawked their wares, their begging, their murmured conversations all blended and formed a vast sigh that was purely Indian.

Sometimes Scotty looked longingly at the fresh food offered by vendors on the station platforms, but those foods were not safe. Even the water wasn't safe, and they had to drink the stale, warm, boiled water provided for passengers. When they ate, it was sparingly, and from the boxes of rations. Occasionally Zircon did permit them to buy a little fruit, but they had to peel it so thoroughly that there was little left but the stones.

They did not talk much. It was too hot to think about things to say. Rick and Scotty slept as much as they could, for sleep was their only escape from the heat, the dust, and the monotony.

"Rick! Wake up! Hit the deck!"

It was Scotty, standing over him and fully dressed.

"Where are we?" Rick asked.

"Nepal. The end of the line."

Rick jumped to the window. The long journey was over! The tracks had come to a dead end against the side of a mountain. There was a ramshackle wooden station and a white-roofed building beside it. And noise. The crowd was waiting again.

But this crowd didn't sigh like the ones of India. This crowd growled. They were all men and dressed in strange, padded clothing that looked like tailored quilts. Their feet were wrapped in bulky, bandagelike coverings and lashed tight with thongs. Their faces were swarthy and all of them seemed to be exactly the same height, as though a blight had stunted them simultaneously.

And beyond, like a great curtain, stood the mountains of Tibet!

Each one in the party reached for his quota of the baggage and hurried toward the door of the train. Rick was the first to step to the ground, and as he did, the growl of the crowd rose in crescendo and moved in on him. He gave Zircon and Weiss a hand with their baggage, and soon the four were standing in the center of the mob on the platform.

"One of us will have to supervise the unloading of the equipment," Zircon shouted above the din.

"I'll do it, sir," Scotty offered, and pushed his way back toward the compartment.

"Looks like they all want to work for us," Rick commented, scanning the avid faces.

"We'll pick no guide from this mob," Zircon answered. "I'm to see the Tibetan border official here."

The scientist began pushing through the closely packed, noisy crowd and Rick followed him to the official-looking building beside the station. Weiss went back to help Scotty.

Zircon took the four passports from his pocket and walked through the door marked *Customs.* It took a moment to become accustomed to the dimness, but they finally located a cubbyhole of an office at the end of the gloomy hall.

A slim figure stepped from the door and bowed. He wore a strangely mixed garb—a wide, blue sash, balloon-sleeve shirt, and striped pants pressed the wrong way. They looked as though they were worn only for official business—and business had been poor since 1923.

"Sars," he purred, bowing again, "could do for you?"

"Yes. I am Professor Zircon," the scientist began.

"Of the Americans party, yes," the man finished for him. "So too bad. I am sorry." He said it in a monotone, flicking his liquid brown eyes from one to the other.

It was difficult to understand these people, Rick thought. They were always sorry for something. He wondered what it was this time.

"Sorry for what?" Zircon asked.

The official bowed low again. "Regards permission for the entry into Tibet. Revoked it were. Suddenly revoked!"

Rick looked at Zircon and for a moment they were both speechless, then Zircon exploded.

"Revoked! Why, look here . . . This is a scientific expedition. We've come halfway around the world! This thing was settled through official channels long ago. It couldn't have been revoked!"

"Suddenly revoked," the official repeated.

Rick looked hard at the man and decided he didn't like him. He resented his abruptness in telling them the bad news—as if he had rehearsed it.

"Look here," Zircon roared. "I must get in touch with your Tibetan government. There's been a mistake."

The official grinned. "No wires . . . no wires to august government."

Rick felt sure the man had been waiting to spring that.

Then his nose detected an odor.

So accustomed had he become to the sea of smells that was India, that he no longer had the habit of consciously identifying each new one. But this odor struck his nostrils and burned.

Menthol!

Into his mind flashed the picture of a menthol-dipped tissue held to a sniffing nose.

It was incredible. They were a thousand miles, half a world away from Bombay, and yet here was a trademark. The unexpected revocation of permission, the story that sounded rehearsed, the very type of man before them—all seemed to be connected, somehow, with the menthol.

The official stared out of the dingy window as though he had forgotten them both completely. Zircon stomped up and down the room, choking with frustration and anger.

Then Rick spoke out of the growing certainty in his mind, turning his back so that the official could not see his face. He hoped that Zircon saw his wink as he said, "If we're going to be delayed, sir, shouldn't we pay off our bearers so that they can return to Bombay?"

"Bearers? What bearers?" Zircon bellowed.

Rick winked again. "Our menservants, sir," he said.

This time Zircon caught the wink, but Rick could see that it meant nothing to him. He raced on, praying that his sudden scheme was going to work.

"There you go, sir, forgetting them again. Why, I'll bet you even forgot to have those large rupee notes changed." He turned to the official.

"Could you change a five-hundred-rupee note?" he asked.

Rick's heart leaped as the man jumped at the bait. "Of course," he purred, and reached into his pocket.

Rick motioned to Zircon to give him the five-hundred-rupee note. The scientist took it from his pocket, cocking his head in bewilderment.

Rick handed the note to the official and then almost snatched the paper change from the man's hand. He held it quickly to his nose and sniffed.

"I knew it, sir," he said. "Smell." He held the money up to Zircon's face.

The money was pungent with menthol.

But still Zircon looked puzzled. "What is all this, Rick?" he demanded.

"Well, sir," Rick answered, "doesn't this entry permission business look like a put-up job to you?"

Light was dawning on Zircon now. He nodded.

"Why is it that this man was able to change our five-hundred-rupee note out of his own pocket? He doesn't make enough money to carry that large a sum around with him, does he?"

Zircon stared at the official. "You mean you think he's been bribed?" he asked.

"Yes, sir. I do," Rick answered. And as he spoke the words, he saw the official edging toward the door and knew his accusation had struck home.

"Just a moment," Zircon bellowed. "Is this boy right?"

"No, sar."

Zircon took a step toward the man. "Well, I'm going to take a chance that he is and report you to your superior. He'll not only have you discharged, but he'll take every cent of the bribe from you for not splitting it with him!"

Rick realized at once that Zircon could not have chosen a more effective threat, for the man immediately began bowing and purring.

"Perhaps forgot," he said. "Perhaps overlook."

He shuffled over to his ratty little desk and opened

a drawer. As he did so, a look of exaggerated surprise suffused his features.

"I make mistake," he beamed, and held out an official-looking document. "Now I stamp passports." He imprinted them with a heavy seal.

Zircon snatched them from his hand and flashed a triumphant look at Rick.

"I should have you beheaded!" he bellowed, and started from the office.

"Wait, sir," Rick called. "What about the man who gave him the bribe? And the menthol?"

"No bribe," the official demurred softly.

"The menthol proves nothing," Zircon said from the doorway. "Besides, it would take a week to wring the information from this fellow. We haven't time."

Rick realized from the look on the official's face that he realized this fact full well. With the passports, the white men probably would be willing to go off and leave him with his loot.

Rick glared at the man and reluctantly followed Zircon out of the building.

"We'd probably save ourselves a lot of trouble if we found out who gave him that bribe, sir," he said. "And why."

"If we did find out, what could we do about it?" Zircon asked flatly.

"Yes, what could we do?" thought Rick.

But that odor of menthol. It was there, and whether Zircon thought so or not, Rick was convinced that the perpetrator of all their troubles had given himself away.

Hendrick Van Groot!

He was the man who had stolen their equipment, ordered it pushed into the sea. The man who sometimes traveled under the name of Conway. Rick felt sure of it now. But why had he done all this?

Rick followed Professor Zircon back toward the crowd at the railway station, and at the sight of the big man, the yells of the mob increased in intensity.

"Now I'll have to use my own judgment about a guide," Zircon said. He stared at the multitude of natives, all clamoring for the job as they massed about him.

Weiss hurried to his side. "How do you get these devils quiet, Hobart?"

Zircon scratched his chin, then cupped his hands to his mouth and shouted for quiet.

They screamed louder.

Weiss yelled something first in Mongol, then in a strange gibberish.

The tone of the mob rose to a higher pitch.

Then Scotty stepped forward. "Allow me," he said. He put his fists on his hips and yelled at the top of his lungs.

The crowd hushed like a slowing victrola record and was still.

"A miracle!" Zircon exclaimed. "What did you say?"

"Not a thing," Scotty replied, grinning. "It's the face you make that counts, not the words. An old top sergeant's trick."

"I swear if we pick one of these men, the others will kill him in sheer resentment," Weiss whispered.

The bulky little men were staring at Scotty and the other three with fierce eyes.

"I wish I knew how to go about this," Zircon said.

Then his problem was solved for him. Out of the crowd, where he had been squatting unseen till this moment, stepped a huge man who towered above the other applicants. Even Zircon looked small beside him. One eyelid drooped half-shut, giving him a sly, knowing look. His tangled black hair mounted to a peak. He was almost humorous in appearance except for the stringy, black mustache that curved in a sinister parenthesis about his wide mouth.

He tapped his chest with a beefy hand, folded his arms and announced: "Me Sahmeed. Number One guide boy."

The party could not suppress grins and it seemed to amuse this hulk of a man. He grinned, too, and his teeth were like a picket fence with a few staves knocked out.

"Much Number One strong," he grunted, and in two steps he was beside the equipment piled on the platform. Before anyone could stop him, he had lifted the very biggest of the boxes and with barely a shiver of the arms, held it high above his head, tossed it in the air as the party winced, and then caught it again. He lowered it easily to the ground and smiled.

Rick felt like applauding, but he could see that Zircon was not quite convinced.

"Do you know Tengi-Bu plateau?" he asked.

Sahmeed bobbed his head. "Much know Tengi-Bu," he replied.

The other strangely clad men in the mob were grumbling now. They wanted to know what decision was being made.

Then Sahmeed turned, swept his arm in a fierce gesture over the heads of the mob, and growled. Even a heavyweight champion would have ducked at the sweep of that oaklike arm.

The crowd moved back.

"I don't think they'd dare try for the job now," Weiss said.

"Well, I guess he's our man, then," Zircon decided, looking the giant up and down. He nodded to him. "But we'll need bearers . . . and animals," he said to Weiss.

Sahmeed had anticipated the need. He was pointing to one after the other of the gnomelike men in the crowd, and they moved to his side. When he had collected thirty of them, he grunted something in an odd gibberish and they trotted toward the railway station. Soon they were leading mules, and animals resembling oxen, toward the pile of equipment, and without orders from anyone started loading the boxes on the backs of the animals.

Rick looked at the spindly legs of the beasts. "Are those things going to carry our stuff over those mountains?" He pointed to the Himalayas.

"They're yaks," Zircon informed him. "The standard beast of burden in Tibet. Very sure-footed. The mules can take care of themselves. too."

They watched the silent, sweating men load the equipment on the backs of the beasts as Sahmeed stood over them with folded arms.

Soon only the biggest of the boxes, the one that Sahmeed had played ball with, was left. It was obvious that the bearers were waiting for him to lift it onto the back of the largest yak.

Then Zircon did a thing that made Rick's eyes open wide.

As Sahmeed stooped to grasp the corners of the box, the scientist stepped to his side and tapped him on the shoulder. The giant rose and the scientist took his place. His broad back bulged as he took the corners of the box and, to Rick's amazement, swung the load high over his head as Sahmeed had done. Then he held it there and smiled into the guide's eyes.

It was the first reaction except a smile that Rick had seen cross the giant's face. His chin dropped and stayed there.

Zircon lowered the box to the animal's back, lashed it tight. Without another look at the giant, he turned and strode back toward Rick, Scotty, and Weiss.

"Just to show him who's boss," the scientist smiled.

The animals were flogged to their feet by the bearers. Sahmeed led the way up a wide road toward the mountains and, with a last look at the civilization they would not see for many months to come, Rick and Scotty fell in behind the scientists.

If trouble were to follow, Rick decided, it would have rough going from here out.

CHAPTER XI

Tibet

THE road stretched ahead and in less than an hour they had crossed the border into Tibet. There didn't seem to be a level inch, so far as the eye could see. The cries of the bearers, urging the animals on, echoed against the surrounding walls of earth that seemed to be narrowing like a funnel ahead.

Suddenly there began to appear strange markings on the rocks of the mountains.

"Om mani padme hum," Rick read slowly.

The inscription was everywhere now, on the lip of a gorge—the painter must have been a human fly to etch it there—again, high against a flat peak.

Rick hurried to Zircon's side and pointed to one of the painted legends. "What does it mean?" he asked.

" 'Hail, the jewel on the lotus,' " Zircon translated.

Rick scratched his head. "And what does *that* mean?"

Zircon laughed. "It is the way the people of Tibet gain merit in the eyes of Buddha," he explained. "They risk their lives in these painting projects to perpetuate his wisdom."

"But there are more and more of them as we go along," Rick said. "How come?"

"We're on the road to Lhasa," Zircon explained. "The holy city of the Tibetans, where sits the boy ruler . . . the Dalai Lama. They pour over this road by the thousands every day, on their way to Lhasa to worship him."

Scotty joined them and they laughed when he referred to the signs and the carved images as "Tibetan billboards."

In the mountains, day was with them one moment and had fled into blackness the next. There was no dusk, and before they knew it, the caravan was tramping in darkness.

Rick heard the shouts of the bearers and the orders of Sahmeed drifting back through the darkness. He almost ran into the last yak in the caravan before he realized they had come to a halt.

"We'll be pushing as fast as we can," Zircon explained. "No point in stopping until we have to."

"We have to, now," Scotty said. "It's too dark to see."

"Where do we sleep?" Rick asked.

"Right here," Weiss answered. "No one travels these roads at night. They're the best place to be."

"Okay," Rick said. "Come on, Scotty. Let's unpack our gear and curl up on Tibet Highway Number One."

Scotty lifted the sleeping bags and the duffel bags of clothing off the pack yak and dumped them on the ground. As he did so, there was a crinkle of paper.

"Barby's present," he remarked. He held it up to his ear and shook it. "What do you suppose it is?"

"I could guess," Rick answered, "but I won't. It wouldn't be fair."

"You're right," Scotty agreed. "Let's see . . . where can I put this . . ."

"Mine's in with the spare parts," Rick said.

Scotty took his flashlight and leveled it at a pack yak who carried boxes of rations. "I'll put it in with this bunch of chow," he decided. "Then I'll know where it is."

"You always know where the food is," Rick jibed. He unrolled the fleece-lined sleeping bag and unzipped it. It was army type, and equipped with an extra cover that could be propped up like a tent in bad weather. No matter how cold it might get they would sleep warmly.

Fires were springing up. The bearers were getting ready to eat. They had brought their own rations, mutton mostly, and bricks of tea. Their water was carried in skins, while the white men had brought canned water from the States in their ration crates.

Sahmeed saw to it that a fire was lit for the scientists and the boys. It burned with a low blue flame, due to some peculiarity of the wood. Bundles of it had been brought along on two of the mules.

Scotty tore open one of the big ration cases and said, "Bacon and eggs tonight. With fruitcake for dessert. Also coffee." He produced the items as he named them.

The ground-up bacon and powdered eggs tasted good, and they ate with appetite, while the bearers squatted over their meals of mutton, boiled rice, and tea.

After the meal, the professors retired at once to their sleeping bags, but Rick and Scotty walked back along the trail and looked at the stars that seemed to press close with icy clearness.

"We're on the roof of the world," Rick said.

"But the stars look the same. There's the Big Dipper."

The constellation was like an old friend, overhead. They watched the stars in silence for a few moments, then went back to their sleeping bags and climbed in.

There was no sound, no cry of bird or beast, and for a moment the very silence kept them awake—but only for a moment.

When dawn came it was suddenly, like a huge light being switched on. The boys awakened to the sound of the bearers preparing the morning meal and to the stomping of the pack animals. They shivered as they crawled from the warm sleeping bags.

The professors were already up, and the aroma of hot tea sharpened their appetites. There were hamburger cakes for breakfast, taken from the big ration boxes, and crackers and a fruit bar.

While the bearers packed the animals, they stood at the edge of the trail, looking down into a gorge that vanished in the morning mist over a trackless valley far below.

Soon the wooden rods of the bearers slapped against tough hide and the animals started their ponderous progress. Sahmeed took his place at the head of the caravan. The boys and the professors fell in behind, and the procession moved on.

It was shortly after this dawn start that Rick pulled up beside Scotty and said, "I thought you were in condition, Sarge."

"So did I," answered Scotty, who was breathing heavily. Then he grinned. "And stop holding your breath so you won't puff, you faker!"

Rick took a deep breath but he couldn't seem to get enough air into his lungs.

"It's the altitude," Scotty told him. "Professor Zircon says we're seven thousand feet up."

Rick whistled.

"And going higher," Scotty added.

Rick looked at the mountains that mounted like stairs before them. "What we need is my Piper Cub."

"Your little baby would never make it over those," Scotty said, pointing at the snow-clad peaks.

Proud as he was of his little plane back on Spindrift Island, Rick had to admit that Scotty was right. His thoughts were beginning to turn toward home when he heard a commotion from the front of the caravan.

"Looks like Zircon and Sahmeed are having a confab," Scotty remarked.

They walked to the side of the two men. As they reached them, Rick heard Zircon ask, "Does this ridiculous path correspond to this line on the map?"

Rick looked toward the path at which Zircon was pointing. It did seem ridiculous that they should turn off this fairly good road onto the narrow, winding path to the left.

Sahmeed, however, was shaking his head in a violent affirmative.

"Tengi-Bu wait there," he said.

Zircon checked the map again.

"Well, the map makers who charted this should know," he muttered. "But it does seem to be doing it the hard way." He folded the map, returned it to his case, and motioned to Sahmeed to carry on.

In the coolness of the mountains, the sun seemed to race on its journey from one horizon to the next, and before he knew it, Rick had counted three such trips by Old Sol.

"Three days. I'm beginning to get used to this thinner atmosphere," Rick told Scotty.

"Me, too. I wish the scenery would change, though."

"That's what you said about India," Rick joked. "Relax. Why, people pay big money for vacations in the mountains."

"Who's kicking?" Scotty answered in a preoccupied way, looking at something far off to his left.

"What are you staring at?" Rick asked.

"A sheepherder . . . I guess." Scotty pointed toward a high cleft in the mountain behind them. "It looked as though he was carrying a bow and arrow."

"I don't see anything," Rick said, shading his eyes.

Scotty squinted and then shook his head. "By golly, he was there, but he's gone now."

"We're probably the first white men the poor old sheepherder ever saw." Rick grinned. "Let him have his peek."

It was plain, as the days wore on, that Zircon was not pleased with the ruggedness of the going. He had expected narrow trails, he growled, but not rat runs. It seemed to Rick that every time they did come out upon a fairly usable trail, the map would indicate a turn and they would be back to clinging to the sides of the peaks.

Then, on the third Sunday of their journey, Scotty saw something again. He pointed behind him, but before Rick could hurry to his side, it was gone.

"It's a mirage," Rick laughed. "Only radar tramps like us would be silly enough to be found in this neck of the woods."

But Scotty kept turning his head to eye the rocks and the ledges behind him. Twice more he called to Rick to look to where he pointed. But neither time could Rick see the figure that Scotty said was there.

Then one day Sahmeed disengaged himself from the head of the caravan. As he walked back toward Zircon, he kept looking down into the valley from which they had just come. He stopped before the big scientist, beckoned him to the edge of the cliff and pointed far down and behind them.

Rick and Scotty hurried to his side and followed the giant's gaze. For a moment Rick could see nothing but dull, brown rock, then suddenly he gripped Scotty's arm. A streak of white had dodged from the shelter of a boulder and ran to the protection of another! It seemed tiny at this distance, but it was a figure, and one that obviously didn't want to be seen.

Zircon looked from Rick to Scotty and then said flatly: "We are being followed."

CHAPTER XII

The Watchers

IMMEDIATELY after the white-clothed figure disappeared, Zircon ordered a double guard on their encampments. Rick, Scotty, and the professors alternated in watching over the sleeping camp. Scotty was sure that the white figure was not one of the figures he had seen previously. The other figures had not been dressed in white.

On the second night after the doubling of the guard, it was Scotty's turn to stand first watch. Rick was dog-tired from the day-long hike, and the moment he stretched out he was asleep. He had no idea how long he had slept or what woke him, but he found himself starting to sit up slowly, not knowing why he was doing it. Had he heard a sound?

He strained to see into the darkness.

Then Rick heard it! Scotty's low whistle—their private signal! Again it pierced the darkness and this time he located it, off to his right.

Grabbing his tiny flashlight, he scrambled barefoot

across the loose rock, gritting his teeth in anguish at each noisy crunch. He almost fell over Scotty in the darkness and with a tremble in his voice whispered, "What is it?"

"I don't know," Scotty answered hoarsely. "Sit here and watch."

Rick eased himself to a sitting position and stared in the direction Scotty had indicated. Little lights began to dance before his eyes as he tried to pierce the darkness.

For a full quarter hour they barely breathed as they waited for some betraying sound. Finally it came.

A sliding sound, then a ripping of cloth and a soft exclamation in the dark. Then quiet again.

"Over there," Scotty said, jabbing his finger toward the curve in the path.

Then they saw it. A white-clothed figure silhouetted against the sky.

"How did he get by the guard below?" Rick asked.

"That's probably his racket," Scotty whispered.

They watched the figure bob up and run behind a rock and then scamper closer to them.

"We are going to take this character with the old school tackle," Scotty whispered.

"You go high, I'll go low," Rick answered. They crouched together.

For a moment Rick feared that the figure had heard them, but it rose again and straightened up. Too far to attack yet, but then he saw a hand stealing into the white robe and his heart leaped into his throat. He had seen knives come out of such robes, and knew they could wait no longer.

Without a sound, Rick's legs buckled and in the next split second he and Scotty were flying through the air, straight for the figure in the darkness.

Scotty hit him at the neck and Rick tackled him squarely at the knees, and the figure bounced like a rubber ball. But their quarry wasn't giving up. Arms were flailing under the white robes and legs were kicking. In a flash, Scotty was astride the prostrate figure and pinioning the arms to the ground.

"The light!" he yelled to Rick.

Rick reached for his flashlight and flipped its switch. Then he turned its beam squarely into the face of the prowler beneath them.

There, staring up into their eyes was a face Rick had thought he was never to see again.

Chahda!

It seemed unbelievable that the native boy could have managed to follow them all the way from Bombay, yet there he was. Rick and Scotty fired eager questions at him but it wasn't until later, over a good breakfast, that they heard the whole story.

Fully aware that all eyes were on him, Chahda sipped a cup of steaming tea slowly and with relish, deliberately prolonging the moment with his natural flair for the dramatic.

Rick grinned to himself as Scotty and the professors shifted uneasily. This, he thought, was Chahda's moment, and the Hindu boy intended to make the most of it.

At last Chahda put the teacup down and smiled at the faces around him.

"Very good tea," he said politely.

Scotty exploded. "Come on! Can't you see we're waiting for you to tell us all about everything?"

Chahda settled himself comfortably. "Is like this." He smiled at Rick. "You remember we talk about the map? How I say is not like what Sahibs in Nepal say?"

"I remember," Rick said.

"You not believing," Chahda accused. "I go away, so quiet no one see, and I go to the house of a *Sikh*. He is old man, this one. When I know him before, he is *Risaldar-Major* in Nepal."

"That's a rank in the British Colonial Cavalry," Weiss supplied.

"He know this Tibet good," Chahda continued. "I think, myself, he know about this map. But he is not home. I am sitted down on the stairs and wait. Such time passes! But does this one go?" He waved his hand in an airy gesture. "Not Chahda! He waits some more."

"Go on, go on," Weiss said impatiently.

"Yes, Sahib. Soon comes the Sikh Sahib, and he is forget me, because I have new clothes, like a *hazoor*. But soon he remembers, and he shows me his maps of Tibet, and I show him the path from the maps.

"He looks and he makes great rumble in his beard, like so." Chahda demonstrated with a low growl. "He says: '*Ayah!* Such a bad thing! How gets the Sahibs such a path?' And I say to him that is sent the maps by the Asiatic Geo . . . Geo . . ."

"Geographical Union," Rick said helpfully.

"Yes. He knows good those people. He takes me to them, and I show the path and they say they make no path like this on the maps for the Sahibs. They draw new on maps, and say, '*This* is the path we draw.'

"My friend give me the new maps, and I am run for the station. But when I come, the train is go. I see Sahib Rick. I make shout, so loud! I make shout: 'Is wrong the maps!' Then the Van Groot Sahib is bang! I am dead. My new clothes is get dirt. Soon I am waking up." He paused dramatically. "Is gone the maps."

"Van Groot!" Scotty exclaimed. "If I ever get my hands on that walking cough drop I'll break his neck! He's behind all this. He must have switched maps. That's why he was so long bringing them."

"I'm afraid it looks that way, Scotty," Hobart Zircon agreed.

"But why?" Julius Weiss asked. "What could he hope to gain?"

Rick answered for all of them. "If we knew that . . ." He stopped. "But we've said that before. Anyway, we know now that Van Groot is behind it. Van Groot and Conway, if there's any difference."

"But Van Groot's route *should* take us to the Tengi-Bu Plateau," Zircon mused.

"Are you sure of that, sir?" Rick asked. "He might have been sending us into a dead end of some kind."

"There is that possibility," Zircon admitted, "but somehow, in spite of the evidence, I doubt it."

"We've only the word of this little boy for it," Weiss added.

Chahda corrected him politely. "Soon maybe sixteen years, Sahib Weiss."

The professor smiled. "Sorry, Chahda. I'd forgotten you were almost grown up. Well, anyway, let's hear the rest of your story."

Chahda accepted a fresh cup of tea from one of the bearers. "Is most short. On next train to Nepal is English Sahib. So much money! Many peoples work for him. I make believe I am Number Three boy, and I ride on train to Nepal. So easy. But when is come Nepal, is no more trains."

At Nepal, Chahda had acquired the long, white, padded coat he wore, just how he didn't explain. Probably "borrowed," Rick thought. Then, with the few rupees left from the money Zircon had given him to buy clothes, he had bought bricks of tea, a tin can for heating the tea, and a kind of compressed wheat. Rice had completed his meager rations, and he had found water wherever he could.

Then he had started out after the caravan, hiking as fast as possible, trying to catch up, and sleeping at night wrapped in his padded coat.

"We owe a lot to this little guy," Rick thought. "Coming after us like that, on short rations, almost freezing at night . . . that's loyalty!"

The Hindu boy continued, groaning realistically. "All time walks. Is sore the foots. Soon I see the Sahibs, but I must go slow, because peoples is watching."

The party exchanged glances. The watchers Scotty had seen!

"Did you get a look at these people, Chahda?" Zircon asked.

"Yes, Sahib Zircon. Once I hide in rocks and one is go by close, and I am almost touch. He is like Chinamens, but not same. He is small, like me, and he is shave the head, and is wear clothes with pads. He is have plates on chest made from . . . from . . . what is called skins from animals, please?"

"Leather?" Rick asked.

"Is so," Chahda assented. "Is also carry a . . . a . . ." He made motions with his hands.

Light dawned. "A bow and arrow!" Rick exclaimed.

Chahda nodded.

Weiss ticked off the points on his fingers. "Small, like a Chinese but not precisely, shaven head, padded clothing, leather armor, and a bow and arrow. Hobart, what does that mean to you?"

"Mongol."

"Exactly. But it's quite impossible. A Mongol such as Chahda describes would have lived five or six centuries ago."

"But he saw one," Rick said.

"So he said. And I doubt that he could have made up such a tale. I'm afraid that we have another mystery on our hands," Weiss sighed.

Rick grinned at Chahda. "Anything else?"

"One small thing. I forget to say this. Before I am taking train, I go back to the Sikh Sahib. He is help. We go to the Geo . . . what you said before."

He reached into his capacious padded garment. "We get these."

He drew out a thick sheaf of corrected maps.

CHAPTER XIII

Dead End

ZIRCON looked from the old maps to the new. "I don't know what to say," he sighed. "From what Chahda has told us, it would be wiser to take this new course."

Weiss spoke up. "I think the evidence is no longer circumstantial, Hobart. Van Groot changed the maps. We should take the new trail."

Rick and Scotty nodded assent.

Zircon rose and said, "Well, if it's agreed that we're going to change our course, I'd better inform Sahmeed." He walked over to where the bearers were just finishing breakfast.

The boys started breaking camp, rolling up their sleeping bags and those of the scientists. Then Rick noticed a disturbance among the bearers. "Now what's wrong?" he asked.

Zircon and Sahmeed were face to face, and the giant guide was waving his arms furiously. It was evident he did not agree with the decision to change the course.

"We'd better lend a hand," Scotty said.

"This beggar is being difficult," Zircon told them when they came up to him.

Sahmeed waved a hamlike hand in the new direction. "Bad! Much bad! No go."

Weiss pointed to the trail they had been following. "Where this trail go?"

"Go Tengi-Bu," Sahmeed declared.

Weiss pointed south, in the direction of the path they were to take. "Where go?"

Sahmeed shrugged.

"I don't think he knows," the little professor said flatly. "I doubt that he has ever been to Tengi-Bu. Otherwise, he wouldn't insist on taking what is obviously the wrong way. No wonder the trail was so rough!"

"This is the last straw," Zircon bellowed. "Do you mean to say you think this beggar lied just to get the job?"

"Maybe he was planted," Rick suggested.

Zircon thought about it. "I don't see how he could have been," he replied. "We picked him ourselves."

"Did we?" Weiss demanded. "Could we very well have chosen anyone else, the way he dominated that crowd?"

Sahmeed had been staring impassively, his arms folded.

Zircon faced him. "Well, whoever he has been working for," he said grimly, "he's going our way now." He pointed in the direction of the new course.

"We go, Sahmeed."

Sahmeed didn't move. He spoke a guttural order. As one man, the bearers sat down. They were refusing to go on!

"*We're* moving," Zircon said. He took the lead line of the first yak. Rick jumped to help, and they began lashing the animals together, head to tail.

Sahmeed's composure broke. He stepped forward and snarled something in his own tongue. The bearers got to their feet.

Zircon smiled. "I didn't think they'd sit quietly if we started to take the animals and all their food."

Sahmeed was bent slightly, his big fists clenched. His face was hard and his eyes glittered.

"Look at him!" Rick whispered. "He won't let us move!"

Zircon whirled to face the big man, and the jacket on the professor's broad shoulders bunched as he lifted his arms.

"No, Hobart!" Weiss said hoarsely.

Then Scotty walked up. He had gone back to the rear of the caravan while they were talking and now held his rifle carelessly in one hand.

At sight of the weapon, Sahmeed's face changed.

Scotty held out a ration tin to Rick. "Put a rock in it and throw it," he invited.

Rick stooped and picking up a stone, dropped it into the can to give it weight. Then, making sure that all eyes were on him, he threw it with all his strength, far up and out.

Scotty watched with seeming idleness as the can

arched into the air. Then, miraculously, the rifle was at his shoulder.

It barked once. The can stopped in its downward plunge and jerked upward. The rifle spoke again. The can jerked once more.

Scotty lowered the rifle and the can fell down the slope.

The muzzle was pointing in the general direction of Sahmeed. "We go, Sahmeed," Scotty ordered. There was no doubt in his tone.

The guide turned slowly and spoke to the bearers. In a moment, they swung off on the new trail.

Rick took a deep breath. "Nice going," he said hoarsely.

Weiss patted Scotty's shoulder silently.

"Now we know the language that brute understands," Zircon said. He walked to the head of the caravan, map in hand.

Chahda, who had not said a word during the entire scene, grinned now and sighed in relief. "Now Sahmeed know who is boss," he exulted.

"But he doesn't like it," Rick observed.

"We watch Sahmeed close," the Hindu boy advised.

Scotty slipped the safety catch on the rifle and smiled. "I'll be right behind him, from now on."

The caravan traveled southward, with Zircon and Weiss watching the map and Sahmeed closely. They were off the trail for long hours until they picked up a wider path that coincided with a secondary route on the new map. Within a day they should reach the well-defined route the Geographical Union had specified.

When they camped for the night, the four white men took turns on guard, Scotty's rifle in their hands. But there was not so much as a word from Sahmeed that night nor in the days that followed.

They were twelve thousand feet up now! Chahda was the first to notice the drowsiness that made everyone feel as though they were sleepwalking. The air seemed thin as gossamer to their straining lungs. Their minds couldn't seem to take hold of ideas or conversation and their tongues stumbled on words. Weiss suffered most, and they were forced to call many rest periods on his account.

"Oxygen starvation," Zircon told them. "I told you it would be fierce up here."

As the sun started to dip into a cleft in the mountains, one evening, Rick realized that they had traveled less than three miles the entire day.

"Pilots wear oxygen masks at this height," Scotty said. "Where are ours?"

Rick grinned. "You'll be wanting piggyback rides next."

"The altitude record is fifty thousand . . . no, sixty thousand feet," Chahda said vaguely. They laughed at the boy's remark. It was the first time he had ever been in doubt about anything from his "Alm-in-ack."

"We'll have to give you artificial respiration pretty soon," Scotty teased the Hindu boy.

Rick plodded on for long minutes before he spoke again. "This weak feeling could be an awful nuisance if Jo-jo decided to get tough." He pointed ahead to Sahmeed.

"He won't," Scotty said. "Not with this behind him," he added patting the cold metal of his rifle.

When they came to a clearing in the trail, Zircon called back that this was to be their encampment for the night. It was still light, but he had decided that the rock-free area was the best they could hope for. Besides, all of them were unnaturally tired because of the altitude.

"I wonder how close we are to Tengi-Bu?" Rick asked, as he sank to the ground.

"Just a few more days, according to the map. We'll make it by the tenth, all right."

"Barring accidents," Rick said.

"Why do we have to go to Tengi-Bu anyway? Why not set up right here?"

Professor Weiss came by in time to hear Scotty's question. "Isn't that the same question Barby asked?" he inquired whimsically. "As a matter of fact, Scotty, doubtless there are locations nearer than Tengi-Bu where we could set up. It just happens that we don't know any of them."

"But couldn't we look for one?" Scotty wanted to know.

"That would be rather unscientific," Weiss laughed. "Can you imagine an expedition like this starting out without a definite destination?" He grew serious. "Actually, there are good reasons why we must reach Tengi-Bu. One is that we have precalculated our angles of transmission. Another is that we know from previous research that Tengi-Bu is electrically suited for the experiment. By that, we mean that the ground has little tendency to absorb radio-frequency signals."

Scotty scratched his head. "That's nice," he remarked, bewildered.

Rick and Weiss laughed at his puzzlement. "I don't know how to explain any less technically," Weiss said.

"Isn't it true, sir," Rick put in, "that we could set up anywhere near Tengi-Bu, if we found a proper location?"

"Yes," Weiss agreed, "but why should we search? We know Tengi-Bu will do." He moved on toward Zircon, who was exploring rations in search of the evening meal.

"This radar business makes my head tired," Scotty complained, "and the hiking to get there makes my legs tired."

"Same here," Rick agreed.

They stretched out flat, too exhausted for the moment even to bother with food.

A snore startled Rick and he sat up. It was Chahda, curled up in the long, white, padded coat he had acquired, and dead to the world.

"It's going to be no fun standing guard tonight," Rick said. "I have the third watch."

They had been rotating the guard, breaking the night into four parts. Tonight, Zircon would take the first hours, then Weiss. Weiss would awaken Rick who would stand watch until it was time to wake Scotty.

"You've got the best deal," Rick continued. "You can

sleep in one stretch, and when you get up you won't have to go back to bed."

Scotty grinned. "Stop beefing. You'll get the last trick tomorrow night."

Rick rose wearily. "We'd better make chow. And wake up Chahda before he freezes to death. It sure is cold up here."

They found Zircon and Weiss together, staring at a cleft in the mountain that towered overhead.

"I told you we had forgotten something," Weiss was saying grumpily. "Binoculars . . . one of the most obvious things."

"It was hard to think of everything," Zircon replied testily.

"What is it?" Rick asked.

Zircon pointed. "We saw a figure up there. It's gone now."

A shiver went through Rick. "The watchers! We haven't seen them for days."

"I'll wager they've seen us," Weiss muttered.

"But who are they?"

"I don't know," Zircon answered. "I've tried not to worry about it, because they've made no move to harm us. I think Sahmeed knows, but he isn't talking."

"It gives me the creeps," Scotty said.

"It is uncomfortable," Weiss agreed. "I hope they're nothing but curious Tibetans too shy to come into camp."

"That seems likely," Zircon nodded. "Yet, Chahda described Mongols. Ancient Mongols."

The sky was fast darkening now. Rick said with false optimism, "The bearers must know we're being watched and they don't seem afraid."

"That's why I'm not especially worried," Zircon said. "Well, let's make supper. I have the first watch, I believe."

Immediately after supper Rick crawled into his sleeping bag. But it seemed as though he had hardly closed his eyes before Weiss was shaking him.

Near by a mule snorted and a yak stirred restlessly. Rick crawled from his warm bed and pulled on his clothes, shivering in the cold. He took a blanket and wrapped it around his shoulders, then sat Indian fashion and tried to keep his head from nodding.

"Everything is quiet," the little professor said, as he handed Rick the rifle.

Silence in Tibet is like silence nowhere else, Rick thought. His imagination peopled the silence with hostile eyes that stared, watching his every move. He shivered again, not entirely from the cold. Who were the watchers?

A yak stood silhouetted against the sky, a low, strong bulk. Rick kept his eyes on the animal and tried to fight off sleep. The thin air made him drowsier than usual. He found his eyes drooping and he jerked upright, but sitting up straight was too tiring. He rested his head against a rock and felt the chill of it through the blanket.

Suddenly Rick was conscious of a funny buzzing sound in his head and his eyes felt parched. His neck had a crick in it.

Had he been asleep?

Impossible. The yak hadn't moved. The moon was still in the same place. He pulled back his sleeve to look at his watch. He had left it in his sleeping bag.

A stone rattled and he grabbed for the rifle.

"Fine guard you are," Scotty greeted him. "I could have stolen the blanket right off you without any trouble."

"Go back to bed," Rick said.

"Go to bed yourself," Scotty answered. "I've had sleep enough. Anything doing?"

"Not a thing." He handed Scotty the rifle and stood up. Around him were the sleeping forms of his friends. More distant were the huddled forms of the bearers, vague shapes in the darkness. The yak he had watched moaned softly.

"Tibet is yours," he said to Scotty and walked over to his sleeping bag. He inched into it, luxuriating in the warm fleece. The next thing he knew Scotty was shouting.

"Rick! Everybody, wake up!"

Scotty!

Rick jerked out of his sleeping bag, wide awake. Dawn was graying the rocks, and Scotty was running through the camp—through an empty camp!

"They're gone," he shouted.

Rick saw that the animals were gone. Only the lone yak remained, still staked in the spot where Rick had seen it during his watch—tied there, so they would be fooled into thinking the rest of the animals were there.

too. The shapes which he had taken to be the sleeping bearers were more rocks!

Sahmeed and the bearers had decamped with all the pack animals except the lone yak!

The professors were out of their sleeping bags now, staring incredulously about.

"But how . . ." Weiss began.

"Look at me," Scotty moaned. "They walked off right under my nose, and I never heard or saw a thing!"

"Wait a minute," Rick said. "I thought I fell asleep last night, while I was on guard. Now I'm sure of it. They did all this while *I* was on the job!"

"Don't be too sure," Zircon contradicted gruffly. "It might have happened to any of us. We'll probably never know. The point is, they've gone."

"The equipment," Weiss choked. "They've taken our equipment!"

"No, sir," Scotty said. "They piled it over there, behind those boulders."

Weiss ran to the equipment and checked it anxiously. "All here," he announced with relief.

Rick walked over to the remaining yak. It was staked next to a pile of ration cartons. "They took most of the rations," he said, "but they left us some. We won't starve for a while."

At the mention of the word, the others stopped short, full realization of their plight sinking in.

Suddenly Rick spun around, remembering. "Chahda!" he exclaimed.

The Hindu boy was gone, too.

"If they've hurt that boy . . ." Zircon began.

"No signs of a struggle," Rick interrupted, "and we didn't hear anything. He must have gone voluntarily."

"If I ever get that big hulk of a Sahmeed in my sights," Scotty said grimly, "I'll blow him loose from his mustache!"

Zircon unfolded his maps and laid them on the ground. The others bent over them. "We'd better have a council of war," he said.

There were no villages within easy range, but beyond the Tengi-Bu Plateau there was a small settlement.

"How far?" Rick asked.

Zircon estimated. "Perhaps two weeks. Depends on the trails."

Rick swallowed. "Two weeks there and two weeks back . . ."

"That means the end of the experiment," Scotty said.

"No," Julius Weiss exclaimed. "We can't let this stop us!"

"Let us be realistic," Zircon said. "Consider, Julius. Heaven knows I don't like the idea any more than you do. But our principal goal now must be to save our own lives."

"Why couldn't we set up the equipment right here and send a message?" Scotty asked.

"They won't be listening for us until the tenth," Rick reminded him.

"What's more," Zircon added, "we could never transmit from here." The sweep of his arm indicated the high mountains close overhead. "We are in a pocket.

Attenuation would absorb our signal, and the mountains would blanket what little did get out."

Scotty looked blank so Rick explained. "Attenuation means that the ground would absorb the signal. That's why we have to get to Tengi-Bu. It's high enough so there's no chance of interference."

"Or somewhere similar," Zircon added. "Any mountaintop would do, but most of these we couldn't climb ourselves, much less carry equipment."

Julius Weiss had been standing quietly, lost in thought. Now he spoke, his kindly face strained. "Hobart is right, boys. Our first thought must be of ourselves. The experiment must wait."

Rick knew what that announcement had cost the little scientist. Has Weiss been alone, he would have stayed with the equipment no matter what the cost. But he felt a responsibility to the others.

The boy tried to reassure him. "It isn't giving it up entirely, sir. We can get bearers and supplies and come back. Dad will keep trying for weeks if we don't answer on the tenth."

Zircon spoke decisively. "We will start for this village at once. Each of us will make a pack of blankets and rations. The rest of the rations will go on the yak."

"Will it be safe to leave the equipment?" Scotty asked.

"We must leave it," Weiss said sadly, "and pray that it will be unharmed when we return."

"If it is," Zircon added, "I will devote the rest of my life to finding Sahmeed. And Van Groot."

It was the calm tone of his voice that made Rick stare. It left no doubt that the big scientist would do just that.

As they lifted the improvised packs to their backs, Rick saw Weiss looking at the equipment, his eyes misty. Then the little scientist fell in step behind Zircon, who was leading the yak. For two years the scientists had dreamed of this project. Now July tenth was almost here and they wouldn't be set up to send the Spindrift message.

As they plodded along, Rick kept thinking of the Hindu boy. "They must have kidnapped Chahda," he said to Scotty.

"I don't think so," Scotty objected. "I think he went voluntarily."

"But why?"

"Maybe he saw what the end of this would be, and figured he would pretend to play along until the bearers reached Nepal. That way, he could organize a rescue party and come back for us."

"That must be it," Rick agreed. "I hope Sahmeed doesn't get wise."

"When he gets in a tight spot he'll probably look in his 'Worrold Alm-in-ack' and talk them out of it," Scotty said.

Rick's thoughts returned to their own problems. Zircon had said that the village on the map was at least two weeks away. He hoped grimly that the food would hold out. His head was down and he almost bumped into Scotty ahead of him as the tiny procession came to a sudden halt. He looked up and stared straight into a wall of rock that blocked their path.

"Dead end," Zircon said hollowly.

It seemed that the fates were spacing their misfortunes with diabolical timing. There was no way around the wall of rock.

"Are you sure we made the right turn back yonder?" Weiss asked.

Zircon consulted the map. "So far as I can see, we're on the right trail."

Rick bent back as far as he could and looked at the steep walls hemming them in. Suddenly he pointed. "There's a path leading up the side of that wall," he said.

The scientists examined the mark in the rock which Rick had optimistically called a "path." Zircon shook his head. "I, for one, could never climb that," he declared.

"And I wouldn't try," Weiss added.

"Maybe I could climb it and take a look around," Rick suggested. "I might see a way out."

Weiss looked again at the precipitous climb. "It's too dangerous, Rick."

"I'll be all right," Rick assured him. Before the scientists could stop him, he had slipped off his pack and trotted toward the base of the cliff. Grabbing on to a jutting rock, he hauled himself up. Hazardous as the ascent had seemed from the ground, it proved to be even more treacherous when Rick found himself climbing. He tested each foothold before resting his weight on the treacherous shale. There was almost no incline to the rock wall and one slip would be his last. He reached a shelf, turned and looked down. The view brought a sick feeling into the pit of his stomach, and he decided not to look down again until he had reached the top.

Inch by inch, he wormed his way up the face of the cliff. It took a full twenty minutes to complete the dangerous climb, but at last he hauled himself to the very top and stood on the small square of summit.

He leaned over and looked down, waving to the party below.

"Okay," he shouted and the words echoed back from the mountains.

"How does it look?" he heard Scotty call. That was good. They could talk to each other because of the acoustics of the rock walls. He saw instantly why they had come to a dead end in their supposedly correct route.

A trail of broken rock twisted down the mountain and ended in a doorlike piece of rock on the trail. There had been a landslide and the huge rock had fallen directly across the trail.

Because of his angle of observation, Scotty, Zircon, and Weiss were out of view and he leaned outward slightly to call to them. As he leaned over, his foot slipped forward and broken shale started to clatter down the cliff wall. It was a mere trickle at first, but as the weight of the shower rained against the cliff wall.

Rick felt a rumble and saw to his horror that his slip had dislodged a great slab. It broke off, bounced out from the wall and plummeted straight toward the spot where his friends were standing.

"Look out!" he shouted.

For a moment he didn't dare look down or call to them. Then he heard Scotty's voice. "Halloo-o-o . . . Rick, are you all right?"

He turned cautiously and looked straight down.

All three figures were looking up at him. He let out his breath with a relieved whoosh.

"Yes, I'm okay," he yelled back. "I'll take a look." He could see clearly the country around him and the other side of the cliff. It was much less precipitous on the far side, and as he looked down, Rick saw another trail hugging the cliff on that side. He followed it with his eyes. Far, far down its course, he could see that it joined with the path upon which his friends now stood. In the other direction it seemed to lead straight south, the way they wanted to go. If the three men retraced their steps, they could pick up this path, he decided. It would be a simple matter of following the new one from there on. He measured the distance with his eye and judged by the length of the narrow path that it would take them some time, perhaps two hours, to reach that junction far below.

He waved to them and prepared to descend along the path he had climbed. But he saw at a glance that the sliding shale had sheared away the path. Descending it now would be plain suicide.

He shouted his predicament to the figures below and gave them directions for finding the new path.

"I'll climb down the other side and meet you at the big red boulder down there," he informed them. "It's shaped like a beehive. You can't miss it."

They waved and started down the path, and Rick watched them disappear.

Then he started to descend.

CHAPTER XIV

Strange Warriors

Rick's look at the side of the cliff had been deceptive. The descent wasn't as easy as he had expected. The rock was jagged and cut his hands as he edged his way toward the path far below.

He was forced to make detours of as much as a quarter mile in order to lower himself a few feet. At one point he came to a stretch of the cliff that was glassy smooth. There seemed no way around it, but again he detoured and made a few feet more progress.

He looked at his hands and winced at the cuts in the palms, but he couldn't rest now. He saw that the sun was rushing toward the western horizon and he certainly didn't want to be caught on the face of the cliff at night.

The way looked easier for a short stretch and he was making fast progress for a time. Then he lowered himself to a wide shelf jutting from the cliff, and as he did, the rock he had used as a brace broke off in his hand. There was no danger of his falling off the shelf, but when he looked up, he realized that he couldn't retrace his steps. And the shelf stuck too far out to enable him to lower himself from it.

He was trapped!

He searched the wall frantically for some way out of his predicament. Above him, it was smooth. Not a finger of rock existed for him to grasp, to retrace his steps.

The shelf was strewn with rocks of all sizes, relics of the hundreds of landslides that had occurred in these mountains. Toward the end of the shelf was a big boulder. Rick grasped it and leaned far out. The wall beneath it was steep, but there were lots of rocks sticking out. If only there were some way to lower himself to one of those rocks! He couldn't grasp the edge and drop. It was too crumbly. He fingered his belt and a plan formed in his mind—if he dared try it. But he had to!

His fingers shook as he unbuckled the belt. Then he took another look below and his heart sank. Even if he could moor the belt to something, it was still not long enough for him to reach safety, below. If only he could lengthen it! He stripped the light windbreaker from his back. He looked at the seams of the arms, tugged hard at them and then yanked with all his strength. The seams held.

Thanking his lucky stars, he tied the ends of the sleeves together. He looped the belt around the knot in the sleeves and had a continuous length of double sleeve and belt.

If only the boulder were heavy enough, Rick prayed. He pushed at it and though it teetered slightly, he could not move it. The boulder would serve.

He draped the body of the jacket around the boulder as he would around the shoulders of a chair. Then he pulled on the belt and the arms stuck straight out from the boulder. If only the arms were long enough to give him the extra foot or two he needed!

Looking down from the shelf, he gulped, tested the improvised lowering rope and slid toward the edge. At the first jerk of his weight upon the odd arrangement, the rock teetered and terror shook Rick. But it teetered only an inch or two, and held.

The belt was smooth, and he was glad he had wrapped it around his hand. Inch by inch, he lowered himself toward the outjutting rocks beneath the shelf. His toe plucked out at one of them. He was almost at the end of his life line now. And as he hung there, ready to let out the last few inches of the belt, he realized that he would never have the strength to pull himself back up again.

It was now or never.

The end of the belt was reached, and he saw that he could not quite touch the rock toward which he had been aiming. He didn't dare drop the last few inches, for he knew he could never hold his balance on that miserably small rung of rock.

His palms were perspiring, and his head was just below the edge of the shelf. Then he spied another rock, jutting out slightly beyond the one below him. It was about table-top size, and it would need a swing to get to it, but he had to try.

He started his body swaying like a pendulum, in toward the wall. It was taking the last ounce of strength from him and he knew he couldn't hold on much longer. With a last, convulsive jerk, he swung free.

His feet landed squarely on the rock.

He grabbed for the wall with feet, knees, fingernails . . . then he collapsed against its face.

For a full minute Rick lay there, breathing heavily. Then he looked straight down at what had lain in store for him had he slipped. His friends would never have recognized him after those razoredge rocks had finished catching him on the way down . . . if they had ever found him.

He looked at his wrist watch and realized with a shock that four hours had elapsed since he had started to descend from the top of the cliff. It looked like another three to the ground.

As he dropped to the path and looked up at the course he had followed it seemed incredible that he had made it, but there he was, safe and sound. The red rendezvous rock agreed upon was off to his left, and he headed in that direction.

Distances were deceptive, he soon discovered. From the top of the cliff the red boulder had not seemed terribly far away, but as the minutes ticked off and he did not come to it, he began to get panicky. He felt terribly alone and once stopped and yelled at the top of his lungs.

The echoes laughed back at him.

He tried calling his friends' names.

There was no answer.

No reason why there should be, he told himself. They were probably still looking for this path. What if they didn't find it? What if they got lost? What if he never saw them again?

He tried not to think of the answers, and hurried on as fast as the narrow pathway would permit. He looked down at the drop that fell away below him. He had forgotten what level ground was like. He would walk with a lean to the left for the rest of his days, he decided.

And then he heard a sound.

It was not mortal, he told himself. Probably an echo, but he stopped to listen. There it was again, and it *was* mortal.

A laugh! But a strange laugh. Not Scotty's. And certainly no laugh like that had ever come from Weiss or Zircon. It was low and throaty, and if a laugh could be cruel, this one was cruel.

He was so startled that he couldn't tell from which direction the sound had come and he started running one way and then stopped and headed the other way, in panic.

Why should he be frightened? Rick asked himself. If anyone were near, he wanted to see him, to ask his aid.

But some instinct raised the hair at the nape of his neck and he knew he must dodge this voice at all costs.

He looked wildly about, searching for a hiding place. Far ahead, he saw a hole in the wall, about six feet up.

But what if the voice were coming from that direction?

He had to chance it and he ran.

The voice *was* coming from this direction, and now he heard more than one! He heard them coming closer and he knew that only a miracle would keep him from being seen. They were just around the curve that shielded him from them.

His hands grabbed for the rocks that seemed placed beneath the hole like ladder rungs and, faster than he would have believed possible, he hauled himself toward the hole and into it.

And then, four of the strangest-looking men he had ever seen, came into view below him.

They were short, and their heads were shaven. They wore leather armor and helmets and each carried a spear, tipped with some coppery metal. They had wide, cruel mouths, and their faces were yellow and oily and their eyes slanted. They reminded Rick of something he had once seen in a book . . . warriors of another age.

And then one of them reached for the rock below Rick's hiding place and he realized with horror that the men were about to enter the very hole into which he had fled.

He stared about him in the darkness and knew from the draft that the niche was bigger than he had suspected when looking at it from the outside. He could hear even his breath echoing in its confinement, and he plunged into the darkness. The light from the entrance helped him find his way for a short distance, but soon he had to resort to his sense of touch to feel his way along the walls.

As long as he moved, he was staying ahead of these strange men. Instinct told him not to stop moving. Night had never been darker than the trap in which he found himself. It seemed to push against him, and then the wall fell off from his hand and he found himself groping for it in the dark.

"Must be a hole in the wall," he thought, and started crawling toward it.

It was a narrow niche in the cave that cupped off from the main passage. If the strange warriors were without torches, he might escape detection. He crouched there, digging his fingers into his thighs, listening to the footsteps coming closer and closer.

Then, there was the smell of rancid oil next to him and a heavy foot, inches from his body, and he recoiled.

The other men were close behind, but they, too, passed and he heard them shuffling ahead. Then the sound faded in the darkness.

When he considered it safe, he rose to his feet and made ready to retrace his footsteps to the path outside.

But something made him stop.

Those men . . . where were they going? They had seemed very familiar with this cave, if it was a cave. It could be a passageway. But to where?

Rick stood uncertainly in the dark. If those men were going toward civilization, it would be worth taking the chance of following them and finding out if that civilization could be of help to him. Scotty, Zircon, and Weiss would wait for him at the rendezvous. Besides, if they were anywhere near, they would have heard his shouts.

He felt for the wall again and started inching his way along in the inky blackness. Suddenly he saw a sliver of light and as he turned a curve in the passageway, it turned to bright sunshine.

Though there was no sound from the leather-armored warriors, Rick crept cautiously toward the source of light. He came out upon a narrow ledge. Rude stone stairs dropped away below him. They twisted and turned down the face of a long mountain slope, and there at the foot of the steps was the most unbelievable sight Rick had ever seen.

A lush, green valley spread before his eyes. Studding it were obelisks and towers of a thousand hues. Cultivated fields and houses that dotted the valley in neat rows made a patchwork of exquisite beauty.

And then he realized who the men were that he had seen, and what he had stumbled on. He heard again the words of Zircon, when Chahda had spoken of seeing the men who had been tracking them, many days ago. The men Chahda saw had been dressed in the same attire as those Rick had just seen.

They were Mongols, Zircon had said, but of a kind considered dead for hundreds of years.

But they were not dead! Their city stretched before him.

A lost city of the ancient Mongols!

CHAPTER XV

The Lost City

THE Mongol warriors had disappeared. Rick stepped cautiously from his shelter and looked down into the city.

It was breath-taking, a city of gold and alabaster, set in a gigantic natural cup in the mountains. The valley was almost square, hemmed in on four sides by sheer walls of rock that soared in broken crags up to the heights. And right across the center of the square valley was a high, man-made wall of a white stone that glittered like granite.

The opening in which Rick stood was almost a hundred feet above the level valley floor. He followed the crude, stone steps down, keeping close to the inner wall and watching his footing.

At the bottom, the path forked. He debated, then turned left. There was no sign of the Mongols.

The city lay before him. Wide, stone-paved streets branched off in geometric patterns between squat, stone buildings of the same white stuff of which the high barrier wall was made. He stood still for a while, watching for some sign of life. But there was none. The city seemed deserted.

He went to the nearest building, moving on tiptoe, afraid to break the silence that lay over the city like a tangible thing.

It was a square building, flat on top, and it had neither windows nor doors. On its side were inscriptions in a language he could not read. The script was Oriental. The stone was rough and cold to the touch.

He was conscious that he was sweating. At first, he thought it was his nervousness and the eerieness of the place, but then he realized that the valley floor was warm. He guessed that volcanic action must lie close under the surface.

The wide street beckoned and he went down it, between rows of the strange, squat buildings. Soon he saw that the street led to a central shaft that rose like a golden needle from between the square structures. It looked like gold, but surely nothing so big could be made of precious metal. At its tip was a torch, cunningly carved from some red mineral.

Rick moved slowly, afraid to let the sound of his footsteps break the crushing silence. He half expected a silent, fearsome horde of Mongols to rise out of the very ground. His imagination peopled the stone buildings with savage beings who watched as he strode down the street.

So strong did the feeling become that he turned aside

and walked to one of the buildings. This time he found a door, and peered in. A face leered at him and his blood turned to ice until he saw that it was a mask. Around the walls were stacks of leather armor, helmets, bows. He steeled himself to enter and went into the gloom. Nothing moved. No living thing inhabited the place.

He went back into the open air and continued on toward the central spire. As he walked, he kept turning his head from side to side, watching, waiting, poised to run at the slightest sign of movement.

He reached the tall needle and saw that it was the very center of the city—on his side of the barrier wall, at least. The golden spire rose out of another of the squat buildings, and the walls of the base were embossed with the same metal as the obelisk itself.

Something about the thing made his skin crawl. He saw the Oriental script engraved on the base of the spire, but this time it was a single word. He touched the golden metal and it was smooth and cold. He took a jackknife from his belt, opened the blade, and cut into the metal. It scored easily, and a thin shaving curled off.

His eyes widened. Soft! Soft as . . . as pure gold! He tucked the metal shaving into his pocket and walked around the base. There were doors in this one, but they were closed and he was reluctant to open them.

He left the central shaft and walked along the deserted streets to the barrier wall. It rose thirty feet into the air, a glittering, unbroken surface. He went along it, looking for some opening. He came to the mountainside without finding one. If only he could scale the wall.

The Mongols had gone somewhere. They weren't on this side of the wall; likely the fork in the trail led to the other side, around the opposite end of the wall.

His searching eyes discovered a place where a rock had crumbled. He might be able to climb up at the spot where the barrier fitted into the mountainside.

He took the first steps, clinging precariously to broken rock. It could be done. He gritted his teeth and went on up. As he neared the top, something gave under his foot. He made a wild grab for the top and his fingers caught on the ledge. For a second he dangled, then his groping feet found new footholds and he lifted himself to the top of the barrier, pulled himself to the flat, wide surface and lay quietly, his heart pounding madly.

The barrier was ten feet wide at the top. He crawled to the opposite edge—and looked down into another city!

This was a living city, filled with people who were replicas of the Mongol warriors he had seen! It stretched out from the wall in row after row of buildings. A huge two-storied building of white stone was the central point on this side of the wall.

Beyond the buildings were gardens, and he caught a glimpse of sheep grazing. At the far side, near the mountain wall, rose a strange, flat-topped hill, a plateau of brown rock that was all of two hundred feet high. The huge table of rock dominated the part of the city next to the mountain wall.

Almost directly below him, a group of Mongols were cooking meat in a pot over live coals. He drew back, afraid of being seen, but no one looked up. At first he thought the entire city was populated by men, then he saw that a good half were women, dressed in the same loose trousers, the same padded coats the men wore.

Warriors strode by with long, curved knives tucked into their belts, and carrying bows. Once he saw a man with a hooded falcon on his wrist.

It was like a dream. Rick felt as though he were suspended halfway between earth and sky, looking down on history.

For long minutes, his fascinated gaze explored the teeming city, and then he stirred reluctantly and drew back from the edge of the wall. The professors and Scotty would have to know about this, if he could find them again.

In a few moments he was on the ground again, heading back to the valley entrance. He shivered a little now, because the sun was rapidly dropping out of sight, and the chill of dusk was setting in. Traveling with long, free strides, watching for a sign of the Mongols, he passed through the dead city. The tunnel opening loomed and he hurried into it, then slowed his speed because it was very dark inside. His footsteps echoed and re-echoed, and suddenly the short hairs on his neck tightened as he sensed an alien presence in the cave. He stopped, holding his breath, and listened tensely.

That strange odor was in the air again, a mixture of leather and rancid butter. He turned slowly to look back the way he had come, and a shadow blocked the dim light from the valley entrance—a shadow that moved!

His heart came up into his throat and choked him. Moving with frightened caution, he felt his way to the wall of the tunnel. Was it imagination, or could he hear heavy breathing? His groping hand searched for the cold rock of the wall—and touched warm flesh!

Rick gave a wild yell and leaped forward, but something struck him from behind, just above the knees and he went down with a jarring thud.

He rolled over, clawing at the thing that held his legs in an iron grip, and his hand found coarse, oily hair. He jerked, and the cave echoed with a cry of pain.

Clutching hands found his arms and pinioned them. Other hands lifted him to his feet. He was rushed back the way he had come, and pulled out of the cave into daylight once more.

Four Mongol warriors held him captive.

Rick looked into the greasy, Oriental faces with their black, animal-like eyes and knew he could expect no mercy.

"All right," he said. "You've got me." He forced his voice to a semblance of calmness. He did not want these evil little men to know how terrified he was.

They let go of his arms and stepped back, drawing curved knives from their leather harnesses. One of them motioned for him to start walking down the path. They fell in around him, two in front and two behind.

Rick walked slowly down the trail and turned to the right at a prod from one of the guards. They were taking him into the occupied part of the city.

Why hadn't he been more careful? They must have

known he was coming, because they had lain in wait in the very niche where he had hidden from the first patrol. But how could they have known? If any of the Mongols had seen him in the dead city, or on the wall, surely they would have raised a cry.

And then there was no more time to wonder, because they rounded a corner of the barrier wall and stepped into the occupied city, and at the sight of him, Mongols came running, yelling to each other. In a moment, a crowd had gathered, hemming him in. An angry crowd, all talking and screaming at once.

Rick kept his head high, but there was cold fear within him. They were yelling for his blood. He could hear it in the shrill, angry voices, and see it in the fierce yellow faces.

The guards pushed their way through the mob, protecting him from hands that reached out to strike him. A foot at a time, shoving back the pressing Mongols, they marched him toward the white central building. The rancid, animal stench of the crowd made him feel sick. Sweat streamed down his face and into his eyes, but he didn't dare lift a hand to wipe it away.

Then, miraculously, it was quiet. They had gained the sanctuary of the big white building.

The guards led him into an enormous chamber of white, marblelike stone. They marched across the stone floor, their footsteps echoing from the walls.

At the far end of the chamber he saw a raised dais and a throne of gold and white, guarded by two Mongols who wore crested helmets and carried long spears.

His guards marched him to it, stood him directly before the throne, then stepped behind him.

"They're waiting for the boss to pass sentence on me," Rick thought. He had no doubt of what that sentence would be.

There was movement behind him. He half turned his head, and saw a Mongol in a yellow robe lighting the torches that stood in cressets along the walls.

Then, behind the throne, the curtains parted. Rick sensed that the Mongols behind him were prostrating themselves.

The man who came out from behind the throne was over six feet tall, gaunt as a skeleton, and the torchlight flickered and gleamed from a skull as barren and polished as yellow ivory. He was incredibly old. His face was a wrinkled saffron mask from which two eyes blazed, and his lips were a thin straight line.

Moving with majestic slowness, he mounted the throne, sat down, arranging the flowing green robes he wore. Then he sat immobile, unmoving and unblinking as a graven image.

Rick licked dry lips and lowered his gaze. He couldn't meet that piercing, unwinking stare.

From behind him, one of the Mongol guards came forward, bowing until his head almost touched the ground. He spoke in guttural syllables, not raising his eyes to the throne. When he finished, there was silence. To Rick, his own breathing sounded explosively loud.

Then the man on the throne spoke, a terse sentence, his eyes on Rick.

The Mongol guard bowed again. He backed away, took a torch from the wall and handed it to one of his fellows. He took Rick's arm roughly and thrust him toward a door that loomed black in the wall at the end of the room. They led him down a passage carved from the rock itself. His heart almost stopped when the faint torchlight showed him grinning skulls set into niches in the rocky walls.

For a full two minutes they pushed on into the dark passage, then they rounded a corner and he saw a faint glow of light. In a moment they walked into a high-ceilinged room that evidently had been a natural cave. He blinked in the sudden light of myriad torches, then as his eyes became accustomed to the glow, he let out a hoarse cry.

There, in a barred niche on the opposite side, were three men. He pulled away from his guards and ran to them.

Scotty, Weiss, and Zircon!

For a heartbeat, the three stared at him and he at them, then Scotty broke the silence.

"Tough luck, kid. We were hoping they wouldn't get you."

Rick found his own voice. "But how . . ."

"Later," Scotty said. "Better watch those gooks behind you."

Rick whirled. The knives were out again, and four pairs of eyes were on him, waiting for the slightest move toward escape. One of the guards went to the niche and pulled out the iron rods that held the door closed. He motioned Rick inside.

As Rick walked in to join his three friends, he tasted the bitterness of despair. With all four of them imprisoned, there would be no means of rescue. Hope was dead now.

The barred door clanged shut behind him. Two of the Mongols took up stations in the room outside, and the other two left.

"Are you all right, Rick?" Professor Weiss asked anxiously.

"Of course he is," Zircon tried to sound reassuring.

Scotty put an arm around his shoulders. "How'd they get you?"

Rick outlined his story quickly, then asked, "What happened? I was hoping . . ."

"That we were still free?" Zircon smiled grimly. "I wish we were. But we blundered right into their hands."

"It was that blasted yak," Scotty said unhappily. "We followed the trail you pointed out, and we got to the red rock, all right, then a hunk of rock fell and hit the yak and he got scared and ran, with us right after him. He got trapped in that little pocket right below the entrance."

"Scotty saw the opening in the rock," Julius Weiss added. "We decided to look into it. Pure curiosity."

"I wish I hadn't seen it," Scotty said. "We went in, and came out in the city. The professors were all excited, of course. I had a hunch we ought to beat it, but it seemed like too good a chance to miss, especially since the place looked deserted. We went down and found that golden tomb. Only, while we were prowling around, a bunch of those yellow monkeys came up behind us. They hit us like a charging backfield. I didn't even have a chance to get my rifle up and cocked."

"They took us without a struggle," Zircon added. "Before we knew they were even there, they were swarming over us like ants."

"I think they saw us as we came through the tunnel," Julius Weiss said. "I'm sure they have had us under surveillance for days."

Rick looked at their prison. It was a corner of the cavernlike room, a network of iron bars rising from floor to ceiling and from wall to wall. There was no furniture.

"Now what?" he asked.

Before anyone had a chance to answer, Scotty held up his hand. "I hear footsteps. Someone's coming."

Instantly all of them were watching the dark opening across the room that marked the passageway. Outside the barred cage, the guards came to attention, faces toward the passage.

The footsteps echoed hollowly in the silence, the footsteps of only one man. Rick blinked his eyes a couple of times, because the uncertain torchlight made him sure he had seen something white, just beyond the rim of light.

Then the four of them gasped simultaneously as into the torchlit room, smiling, immaculate in white linens, a mentholated tissue to his nose, stepped Hendrick Van Groot!

CHAPTER XVI

Conway Shows His Hand

IT WAS Van Groot who broke the shocked silence. He came across the room, leaned against the bars, and said cordially:

"Gentlemen, I welcome you to the Valley of the Golden Tomb."

Zircon spoke first. "I'd enjoy getting my hands on you, my friend."

Van Groot smiled. "Please don't make the mistake of trying it, Professor Zircon. Subotai," indicating the younger of the two Mongol guards, "would be most happy to plant his knife between your ribs. In fact, you have me to thank that you weren't killed outright."

"Explain yourself," Weiss demanded harshly.

"Of course. You met Chepe-Noyan in the throne room. But for my intervention, he would have had you executed at once. However, I persuaded him that we must delay the happy moment for a while—until I had an opportunity to find out just how much you have discovered."

"About what?" Rick asked.

Van Groot chuckled. "Am I to gather that you have no idea why so many things have been happening to your expedition?"

"No idea," Weiss said tiredly. "I suppose it's too much to ask for an explanation . . ."

"Not at all," Van Groot replied, smoothly. "Under the circumstances, I believe a partial explanation might amuse you."

Rick and his friends pressed close to the bars to hear what the man had to say.

Van Groot crumpled a tissue and tossed it aside. "You were unfortunate enough to enter the forbidden part of the city. Entering at all was bad enough, but coming through the Tomb area . . ." He shrugged. "Chepe-Noyan was quite annoyed, and quite definite about your punishment."

"By the forbidden part," Zircon asked, "I take it that you mean the deserted part beyond the wall?"

"Exactly. When you entered that portion of the city, you violated the Tomb of the Genghis Khan!"

Rick's eyes widened. That was why the place had been deserted, why the golden spire dominated that entire part of the city. "That golden monument must be the tomb," Rick said.

"The Golden Tomb of the Great Khan," Van Groot agreed.

"That is ridiculous!" Weiss exploded. "Why, the Khan was buried in . . . in . . ." He stopped suddenly.

"You see?" Van Groot smiled. "The learned professor

has just recalled that no one has ever discovered the burial place of the Khan. According to legend, he was buried in Shansu province, in China. Actually, one of his legions brought his body here and built this city. The people are descendants of his warriors. They guard his tomb against the day when he will return."

"But you," Zircon demanded. "How do you fit into all this?"

"You are," Van Groot chuckled, "looking at the True Messenger of the Great Khan!"

The travelers stared.

"He's insane," Weiss muttered.

"Don't misunderstand," Van Groot said. "That is what they believe. I know better, of course. You see, I was in China some time ago and got into a bit of difficulty with the authorities. I had to leave in rather a hurry. I borrowed a Chinese military plane—without permission, of course—and started for the border of India. However, the gas tanks were not full."

He produced another tissue and sniffed delicately. "Very careless. I should have stolen one with full tanks. At any rate, I passed over the city just as I was running out of fuel. It was a choice of crashing or bailing out, so I decided to jump while near civilization, even though I didn't know the nature of the place. These people had never seen a plane before, much less a man in a parachute. I sized up the situation and it wasn't hard to convince them I was a messenger sent to tell of the Khan's second coming."

"Incredible," Zircon muttered.

"But quite true. I knew a smattering of the Mongol tongue, so it was a simple matter. I'm rather proud of my quick thinking. They accepted me without reservation. Now I can come and go as I please, and they take orders from me. I'm careful not to abuse my power, however. And I'm careful to show proper deference to the tomb whenever I come."

Rick asked a question even though he knew what the answer would be. "Is your real name Conway?"

"Yes, as a matter of fact." Van Groot smiled at him. "You got that name from Meekin, I presume? He never was very dependable. Witness his failures in such a simple matter as wrecking your equipment."

"That brings us to the crux of the matter," Zircon bellowed. "Why have you tried to block us at every step? You had our equipment stolen in Bombay and—"

Van Groot interrupted. "The matter might have ended there had it not been for your two eager young men and the Hindu boy. Your recovery of the equipment almost put a dent in my plans."

"How did you happen to have your hirelings at the dock waiting for us?" Weiss asked. "Surely you couldn't have known that Meekin had failed."

"I knew Meekin had failed when you wired for replacements," Van Groot explained. "I anticipated such a failure, you see, and so I had a clerk at the electronic equipment house watching for such a message. It was ridiculously easy. There was no other place where you could have picked up replacement parts. Then, when you recovered the equipment, I was a bit discouraged, but you played into my hands by asking me to get your maps. I merely substituted others with my own choice of a route marked in. It would have taken you to Tengi-Bu, had you followed it, although in a roundabout way."

"You hired Sahmeed and told him to bulldoze his way into being hired by us," Scotty stated.

"And you bribed the frontier official," Rick added.

"True, to both statements," Van Groot smiled. "I beat you to the frontier by several days, by flying to Nepal. Then I came here and arranged to have Mongol patrols keep track of you. They did very well, until you got separated. We lost young Mr. Brant for a while, but I had Subotai and three men wait in the entrance passage, in case he blundered into the valley. As it happened, they caught him going out after he had already explored a bit." He addressed Rick directly. "You must have come in while your friends were being ushered to Chepe-Noyan by the first patrol."

"Surely others must know of this valley," Weiss said.

"I'm happy to say that you are wrong," Van Groot told him. "We are far off the beaten path, in a country where no one ever ventures. There is nothing to bring Tibetans here, and the Mongols are careful not to be seen when they venture out. They permitted you to see them, on my orders, purely as a means of intimidation. As for the outside world, we are away from air routes and highways. There are no high mountains of the kind that attract climbers. No, I'm afraid we are the only white men who know about the valley."

His voice sharpened. "I regret that you will not enjoy the knowledge for long, but your fate is on your own heads, gentlemen. It was not my plan that you should find this place. I merely tried to keep you away from it. After my attempts on the equipment had failed I decided to let you come ahead, by a route of my choice. But that Hindu boy spoiled things again. I trust Sahmeed has wrung his neck by this time."

"All this trouble to keep us away from here is past belief," Weiss declared. "If I know men of your type, you must hope to gain substantially. Where is your profit to come from?"

"The tomb is made of gold," Rick reminded Weiss.

"True," Van Groot agreed. "But that is not the reason."

"Then what is it?" Zircon demanded.

Van Groot turned and signaled to the Mongol warrior Subotai. The two guards took up stations again at the door. "I'm afraid," he said, "that is one thing you will never know. In fact, my only reason for talking with you now was to see if you did know."

He bowed and walked into the darkness.

The four looked at each other, then Rick sat down on the rocky floor of their cell.

"Somebody pinch me," he said.

"You're awake all right," Scotty told him. He sat down and crossed his legs.

The scientists joined the boys on the floor, and Zircon sighed, "I'm sorry you blundered into the city, Rick. You were our only hope."

"It's a dream," Rick said. "I don't believe any of it." His voice rose a little. "Or are we all crazy?"

"Easy," Scotty said, his hand on Rick's arm. "We're sane enough. Everything Van Groot said made sense."

"Yes," Weiss agreed. "Even the inscriptions on the tomb bear him out. I didn't guess the true story, although I did notice that the word on the base of the monument read *Temujin.*"

"What does that mean?" Scotty asked.

"Temujin was the name of the man usually known as the Genghis Khan," Weiss explained. "Roughly, Khan means leader, or ruler. Genghis Khan is a title that means Ruler of All Men."

"This city would be a great find," Zircon said gloomily, "if we had a chance to report it."

Rick looked at the stalwart Mongols stationed outside the door and remembered how the mob in the city had yelled. He knew, and he knew the others knew, that the Mongols would never let them leave. They would die here, for violating the tomb of a man dead for centuries.

All that Van Groot had said went through his mind. Many points in the mystery had been cleared except the biggest one. What was the man's motive? And why had he wanted to keep them away from here? As Weiss had said, how was he going to profit?

He tried to think of ways to escape, of any source of help.

"Chahda!" he exclaimed. "He's still free."

"Unless Sahmeed has tossed him over a cliff," Scotty said unhappily.

"Julius," Zircon suggested, "tell us about the Genghis Khan."

Weiss demurred at first, then he realized that the big scientist only sought for something to keep their minds occupied, and he began:

"Temujin, whose title was Genghis Khan, was the greatest conqueror the world has ever known. By comparison, Alexander, Napoleon, Hitler—as Scotty would say—were pikers."

The professor's soft voice went on, detailing the fantastic story of the Khan, and little by little the others forgot their predicament, lost in the spell of the tale.

He told of the poor Mongol tribesman who had gathered men around him as a magnet draws iron. He ruled them with a hand of steel, and he taught them his military genius. He took the nomadic Mongol peoples and forged them into a mighty nation of warriors, whose sole business was war.

Then, about the end of the twelfth century, the horsemen of the Khan rode forth in great divisions and swept across the known earth like a flame that seared all it touched. They took India, and all the rest of Asia; they swept into Asia Minor, even into Western Europe. And as they went, the fierce, leather-armored horsemen with their horsetail standards set up a civilization of their own.

Nothing could stop them. They used infiltration tactics copied by the panzer divisions centuries later. They used fifth columnists to penetrate the Great Wall of China and overrun Cathay. They even set up the first pony express, to keep communications going within the Khan's great empire.

And at the head of this mighty force sat Temujin, the

Genghis Khan—the illiterate, cruel genius who measured his campaigns by degrees of longitude rather than by mere nations.

The great Khan died in his seventy-second year, and his warriors took his body to the South, killing every living thing they met on the march, so that his burial place would never be known.

"It was thought," Weiss said, "that he had been buried in China. Now we know the truth. I do not doubt it, because there is proof around us—the name on the tomb, the names of the warriors here. Chepe-Noyan—the old man who is lord of the city—was the name of one of the great marshals of the Khan. Subotai was the name of another division leader."

The professor pointed to the Mongol outside their door. "And there is Subotai. Doubtless a direct descendant of that great warrior who lived eight centuries ago."

"Strange that they should have come to Tibet to find a burial place," Zircon commented.

"Not so strange," Weiss said. "They overran India. In fact, it was a descendant of the Mongol rulers, Shah Jehan, who built the Taj Mahal. My theory is that one of the Khan's divisions came into Tibet and found this valley on their way to India. They would have noted it. A warm, fertile place of this sort is strange in Tibet. Due to volcanic activity close under the surface, I'm sure."

"Why do you suppose it hasn't been discovered?" Scotty asked.

"There is no reason for men to come here," Weiss replied. "There are no villages around. Nothing but rock and more rock. It isn't even on a route between civilized points."

"I guess that's why no planes have spotted it," Rick said.

Weiss nodded. "The place was safe . . . barring an odd expedition like this."

"I was wondering," Scotty mused, "why there weren't any guards at the tomb? They evidently think it's pretty valuable. We looked inside and no one disturbed us until the patrol caught up."

"I imagine they have never felt the need of guards," Zircon replied. "The very existence of the city was unknown and there would be no point in guarding it against themselves. In fact, the entire populated part of the city could be considered a guard."

"I wonder what they'll think at Spindrift on the tenth, when they get no answer?" Rick said gloomily.

"They'll keep trying." Zircon replied. "Then they'll send out a search party. After a while another expedition will come out. There will be a moon relay, you can be sure of that, no matter what happens to us."

"And this city will be found," Weiss added. "It is inevitable."

"Not that it will matter much to us," Scotty remarked.

They fell silent after this gloomy prediction, and presently they picked spots on the hard floor and curled up to rest as best they could, and wait for day.

Who knew what it would bring?

CHAPTER XVII

"They Can Eat Stone!"

RICK couldn't believe that he had slept, but it was the sound of a sword rattling against the cell bars that woke him. Scotty, Weiss, and Zircon were sitting up, rubbing their aching joints. The guard Subotai was opening the cell door.

Dawnlight flooded the outer room from holes in the rock ceiling. The Mongol motioned to them and stood aside.

They filed out and other guards fell in behind them. Subotai took the lead, his weapon in hand. He led them down the corridor through which Rick had been brought the night before, turned the corner, and headed toward the throne room.

As they mounted the stairs, clear daylight almost blinded them and made them blink. Then they were in the throne room, walking toward the aged figure of the leader, Chepe-Noyan.

Van Groot stood beside the old Mongol, immaculate as ever, a mentholated tissue in his hand.

And piled before the throne were many crates—their equipment!

The aged warrior made no move of recognition, but Van Groot said, "Good morning, gentlemen. I trust you spent a pleasant night. As you see, I have arranged for your equipment to be brought here."

Weiss and Zircon looked at it hopelessly.

"Why did you bother?" the little scientist asked.

Van Groot sniffed as one of the warriors moved too close to him. "It might have been embarrassing had a later searching party found these things," he explained. "Of course, it was only a remarkable coincidence that enabled you to stumble into the city, so we have no real fear that anyone else ever will come here."

Chepe-Noyan leaned forward on his throne and began to speak.

Weiss translated under his breath: "We have desecrated the tomb. We must suffer, he says."

Rick, Scotty, and Zircon moved closer to each other.

"Now he seems to be calling on the soul of Genghis Khan to witness his wisdom in dealing with the violators of his tomb," Weiss went on. "I can't understand all of it. It is a sort of ritual speech or prayer."

Watching the face of Chepe-Noyan, Rick knew that there was no such thing as mercy in his code. If anything was to be done, it must be done now. He looked about at the guards, and at Subotai and at another young warrior standing close by their ruler. Every door was barred. There was no chance to make a break. He stared at Van Groot, who seemed as puzzled as Weiss at the tirade issuing from the ruler's lips.

If only Van Groot did not have such a hold over these superstitious people, he groaned to himself. Then he started suddenly.

They were superstitious. Van Groot had proved that by palming off his tall tale on them.

If they'd believed one tall tale, why not another?

He moved closer to Weiss and looked at the throne to see if Chepe-Noyan's eyes were upon them. The aged man's eyes were raised to the heavens as he uttered the imploring tones of his prayer. Subotai and the other guards had their eyes cast to the floor in reverence.

"Professor," Rick whispered, "could we sell this man a story about ourselves?"

Scotty and Zircon moved closer.

"Like Van Groot did, you mean?" Scotty asked softly.

"Yes. Tell them we're messengers from the Khan too, and have delayed identifying ourselves until now to see if they would recognize the signs that our kind bring with us!"

Zircon's eyes widened at the boldness of the idea.

Weiss bit his lip. "How, Rick?"

Rick looked up to see Van Groot looking at them suspiciously, and then Chepe-Noyan's eyes fell upon them.

Before he could speak, Weiss was spouting forth a stream of excited Mongol, pointing to the sky and pounding his chest.

A startled look came into Chepe-Noyan's eyes, and

when Van Groot noticed the reaction and realized what Weiss was saying, he leaped to the ruler's side and began haranguing him from the other side.

But Chepe-Noyan growled at the man, and turned his eyes back toward Rick and his friends.

"By gosh, I think he's going for it," Scotty whispered.

Rick did not wait for skepticism to set in. He ran to the pile of equipment and began searching through it for a square black case, lighter than the rest.

It was right on top. His heart gave a leap as he saw that nothing had happened to his speed graphic.

Chepe-Noyan's eyes were on him now, and Rick knew he had broken the spell of Weiss's words.

"Tell him I will capture his soul in this little box," Rick said excitedly. He slipped in a cut-film holder, set the shutter, and hurriedly guessed at the focus. Guards were rushing toward him. He lifted the camera to his cheek, sighted through the view finder, and clicked the shutter.

Subotai reached for him, his dagger in the other hand. Rick jerked away. "Tell him," he shouted desperately. "Tell him!"

Weiss spoke rapidly.

Chepe-Noyan shouted at the guards and they let Rick go, reluctantly.

Weiss translated as Chepe-Noyan spoke. "He does not believe, but he is a reasonable man, he says. How long will it take to develop it?"

"Just a few minutes. I'll need water."

Weiss passed on the information and a guard was sent from the room.

Rick set up his black velvet hood on its wire frame, then took the developing pans and set them on the floor. He filled them with the bottled, ready-mixed developer and fixative he had brought. When the guard came back with water, he filled the third pan from the gourd, then placed the tent of black velvet over it.

He knelt and thrust his arms through the rubber wristbands.

It was strange to be kneeling, working with groping hands, watching the faces of Chepe-Noyan, the guards, and Van Groot, while his fingers worked frantically.

He took the cut film from the holder and plunged it into the developer. Then he began agitating it.

He was the center of all eyes—fearful eyes.

His friends were afraid the trick would not work.

Van Groot was afraid it would.

The Mongols were afraid, because here was magic they did not understand.

Subotai toyed with his knife, and his eyes on Rick were black and cold, with that strange, animal glint in them.

Sweat stood out on Rick's face and trickled down his nose.

He took the film from the developer and put it into the fixative, almost dropping it. To the watchers he seemed to be kneeling motionless. They couldn't see his hands.

The film would be a negative, of course. But maybe that was good. Chepe-Noyan would see himself as a white image in a frame of mottled grays and blacks, for the Mongol was darker in color than the white stone around him, and the negative was reversed . . . Rick's train of thought broke off. He took the film from the stopper and swished it in the water. It wasn't a good job of developing, but it would serve.

"Now!" he shouted, and pulled his arms free and thrust the velvet tent aside.

He ran to the throne and held the negative up before the Mongol's eyes, so that he might see through it and see that his soul had been captured.

The Mongol shrugged.

Van Groot hid a smile.

Rick turned white.

The film was a solid, formless gray!

Chepe-Noyan's face darkened with anger. He made a disdainful gesture and spoke to Van Groot. The man answered briefly.

Rick turned to his friends. "It's fogged! I . . . but it can't be! The camera is new, and the film was all right."

Suddenly Zircon let out a great roar. "I have it! I know why it was fogged. Radioactivity! I knew there was something familiar about the rock where we camped that last night. It was pitchblende! Radium and uranium ore! Rick, radioactivity fogged your film. Lord, it must be enormously high-content ore!"

He leveled a finger at Van Groot. "That is why you wanted to keep us away. You had discovered a big deposit of pitchblende. You needed time to make arrangements to develop it. Isn't that what you were doing in Bombay?"

Van Groot's smile was gone now. "Yes," he said. "I was working out the details, trying to get mineral rights from the Tibetan government, trying to get backing. I would have succeeded, too! I *will* succeed! Knowing about it will do you no good, my friends!"

And then Chepe-Noyan spoke. Rick saw Weiss's brows lift slowly. It was evident that the ruler's words amazed him.

"We are not to be executed," he translated.

As one, the party relaxed. But what was to be their fate?

Rick could see that Van Groot was as much interested as they were. And as Chepe-Noyan informed them of their fate, he could see that it did not meet with the dapper man's approval.

"We are to be placed on the Hill of the Thousand Repentant Ancestors," Weiss went on, following the ruler's words. "It is the high plateau beyond this building. The reason for this punishment is that, as white men, we may have souls of a different sort."

He quoted the Mongol word for word now. "'No food, no water will be given the prisoners. If they are immortal, they can eat stone. If not, they will starve and die, and their blood will not stain the Valley of the Golden Tomb!'"

When he had finished this pronouncement, Chepe-Noyan rose without another word and parted the draperies behind his throne, signifying that the audience was ended. But Van Groot moved quickly to his side, and Rick could see that he was pleading with the ruler about something.

Rick looked at his friends. It was a relief to know they were not to be killed outright. But was their punishment on the plateau to be any more pleasant than immediate death?

He remembered the barrenness of the plateau he had seen. It towered above the city and on its height a man would be at the mercy of the cutting winds and the rains that swept across these Tibetan peaks. And without food . . .

Suddenly there was a command from the throne. Chepe-Noyan had pushed Van Groot aside and was parting the draperies again. He pointed to the prisoners and spoke a word in Mongol. The guards advanced toward them and with a wave of their flat swords, signified that the prisoners were to start marching!

Rick saw Van Groot's face as he turned to go, and it was white with rage. He turned his head to follow the line of the man's eyes. The rest of the guards were picking up the electronic equipment and carrying it after the party.

They were to be placed on the plateau with all their belongings!

Van Groot's fists clenched and in two bounds he was beside the guards who were removing the equipment. He forced a smile and reached for one of the boxes.

Rick understood his action when he recognized the

box as the one that contained the storage batteries.

The guards paid no attention to Van Groot's movements. And as Rick was pushed out of the throne room, he saw the man carrying the batteries out another entrance.

He gave the matter no further thought for the moment. The guards' prodding swords made anything but moving an impossibility. The prisoners soon found themselves in a courtyard.

Every eye in the party went to the high plateau and traveled up.

The plateau was two hundred feet high, sheer on all sides and with a flat, oblong top about a hundred feet long and fifty feet wide. Rick wondered how they would get up there with all the equipment. But there was no more chance to survey their prison—the swords prodded again and they were marched across the wide grounds.

As they approached the rocky wall of the hill, he saw what appeared to be a tunnel opening in the base. It was blocked by a square stone.

The guards halted them, and two men began to push aside the square rock. Behind the prisoners, other warriors arrived with the equipment.

The rock moved slowly and the opening loomed dark. The air was musty, as though it had been closed for centuries. As the guards motioned them inside, Rick wondered how the place had gotten its name.

A few yards inside, stone steps wound upward through the solid rock. Such a mammoth job of carving would have amazed Rick under other circumstances, but he gave it no thought as they began the long climb.

The Mongols were tireless, and though Weiss was soon breathing hard, they ignored Zircon's plea to let the little professor rest, and prodded the party on. They climbed endlessly through darkness relieved only by a torch in the hands of Subotai, who led the way.

Rick and Scotty waited until the procession had strung out a bit and then moved to Weiss's side and took his arms to help him up the stairs. It seemed as if a whole day had passed, when they finally came to an opening directly above their heads and saw blue sky.

One of the guards had moved levers that lifted a circle of stone from an entrance leading out directly to the flat top of the plateau. He growled at them and they scrambled through the opening.

Julius Weiss collapsed in a heap at the feet of the warrior, and the others lifted him and dragged him to one side. The guards lifted the electronic equipment through the hole in the plateau top and piled it around the prisoners.

Subotai then ordered his men down the stairs again. They saw his cruel face disappear and saw the lid swing shut. It dropped with a thump into the hole, and Rick saw that it was flush with the surface of the plateau. It would be impossible to pry the lid up.

They hurried to the rim of their prison and looked straight down. A crowd of Mongols had gathered about the base and were looking up, chattering excitedly.

Around them, the high Tibetan mountains rose, crouching like glacial sentinels.

There was no way off the Hill of the Thousand Repentant Ancestors—except through death.

CHAPTER XVIII

The Long Night

THERE was no use discussing means of escape, Rick knew. There were none. Their entire prison could be taken in at a glance. It was one flat expanse of rock, broken only by the thin circle that marked the trap door.

Julius Weiss was sitting up now, but he was still breathing heavily.

Rick wandered among the piles of equipment, looking at the labels on each crate.

"I wonder why they brought all this stuff up here with us?" Scotty asked.

"Easiest way to get rid of it, I suppose," Rick answered. "Then they might have been superstitious about it, too." He looked at the equipment idly. "Everything but the batteries," he said. "And you know why Van Groot copped onto those!"

"Afraid we'd send a message?" Scotty guessed.

"Sure. He thought they were our main supply." Rick

snapped his fingers. "But who says we can't still try to send a message? He didn't know about the steam generator."

Zircon looked up. "Without a power supply? We have no water for the steam engine. And without the batteries, we have no filament voltage."

Rick started searching through the equipment. "We still have that little twelve-volt charging unit, haven't we?" he asked.

Zircon rose and pointed it out to him. "There it is. But what can we use to turn it?"

"If we could turn it, would we get twelve volts from her?" Rick asked, reaching for the crate containing the little generator.

"But how can we turn it?"

"Windmill."

The scientist seemed interested for a moment and then shook his head skeptically. "We have the crates so we could make one, I suppose. But what good would it do? The big transmitter takes such a heavy load, twelve volts would do little more than tickle it. I doubt that we could even get the tubes heated properly with so little voltage."

"Well, you know best," Rick said gloomily. "But just sitting here seems like giving up pretty easily."

Weiss rose on his elbows. "Why not try it, Hobart?" he urged. "Who can tell?"

Zircon shrugged his shoulders. "No harm in trying," he agreed. "Let's give it a chance, anyway."

Weiss rose to his feet to help Zircon uncrate the generator, while Rick and Scotty started tearing boxes apart to build a rude windmill.

"Save every nail, we'll need them," Rick said.

Scotty nodded and started making a small pile of the nails beside him. They found a spool and tore the wire from it, deciding to use it as a pulley. A long bolt was chosen as an axle, and the boys decided to use belts for the power drive. Rick's belt was back on the mountain, but Zircon's, added to Scotty's, gave length enough.

Slowly the windmill took shape, and they turned the wooden box staves, serving as blades, into the wind, twisting the blades to give them the proper pitch.

Rick scratched his head when they came to the problem of gearing, but Zircon dropped his work of erecting the radar equipment and came to their assistance. He did some rapid figuring on the gear ratios and picked out the spools in the equipment for them to use.

They stripped the wire from the spools, installed them in the rickety windmill, and then prepared to install the belts.

"Boy, you can't beat a college education, can you?" Scotty joked, as they looked at their masterpiece.

Rick grinned back at him and then looked to see what progress the two scientists were making.

"Well, that's it," Zircon announced finally. He looked out across the mountains as though wondering if such feeble equipment could push a message by them.

"Shall we try it?" Weiss asked nervously.

The boys slid the belts into the pulleys and held their breath. Slowly the blades began to revolve, then faster and faster.

"It's turning the generator," Rick said excitedly.

Zircon bent over the radar modulator and shook his head. "Just as I said," he informed them. "The power's so weak it hardly lights up the tubes."

The others bent to look at the tubes. They were barely glowing.

"And we have no power for our receiver," Weiss added. "Not that it matters. We wouldn't receive anything, anyway."

"Bigger miracles have happened," Scotty said. "They might hear our message and answer."

"That isn't what he means," Rick explained. "Any radar set that picked us up wouldn't be equipped to send messages. That isn't how ordinary radar works. Only the equipment on Spindrift Island and ours here are rigged up to send messages."

"That's right," Scotty remembered. "Regular radar isn't like dots and dashes, is it?"

Rick shook his head. "Well," he said to the scientists, "shall we give it a try?"

Zircon squatted at the key and took a deep breath. Then his fingers began to tap. Weiss's eyes flew anxiously from piece to piece of the strange-looking rig spread out on the plateau.

It was a tiny hope, this attempt to reach the outside world. Blind transmission. If the signal were picked up, Rick mused, no one would be able to tell them it had been heard. That wouldn't matter, of course, if they could send help; but the hope was small.

Zircon was rapping away expertly on the key and Rick's ear picked up the message. He was sending their approximate latitude and longitude and describing their plight.

When Zircon finally tired, he turned the key over to Weiss. The little scientist repeated the message over and over, meanwhile scanning the horizon with his eyes.

The swift Tibetan sun was touching the edge of the peaks now, and night would soon be on them. Rick looked up at the windmill and saw that it was still turning merrily.

"We can send from now till kingdom come, if the wind keeps up," he remarked to Scotty. "Maybe we can send all night."

"I wish I could help," Scotty commented, with a wistful look at the radar key.

"Why not?" Rick said. He took a notebook from his pocket and began to write the dots and dashes of the message that the scientists were sending. "Here." He handed the book to Scotty. "Hold the key twice as long for a dot as you do for a dash. That's all there is to it."

Scotty scratched his head over the scrawl on the page and said he would do his best. "We should stand watches on this thing, don't you think, Professor Zircon?"

Zircon nodded—without much enthusiasm, Rick

noted. Their signal would be pitifully weak at best and he doubted that it was getting out at all.

The black curtain that was the Tibetan night dropped suddenly, and soon it was difficult to make out the figure of Julius Weiss, crouched at the key.

"I'll stand the first watch," Zircon said, "then you can take over, Rick."

"And I'll wake you about dawn," Rick said to Scotty.

There was nothing more to be done. If their message was scaling the mountains that surrounded them, there was a faint hope.

If not . . .

Rick crawled into his sleeping bag and pulled it close about him. There was no friendly chat between him and Scotty tonight as there had been every night on the trail. He knew that Scotty wanted to be alone with his thoughts as he did with his.

They were rambling thoughts, of home and of all that had happened to them. He had a fleeting glimpse of the face of a little Hindu boy as he drifted into the half-world between sleep and wakefulness, and the last thing he heard was the radar key futilely tapping out: *"Held . . . captive . . . high . . . plateau . . . latitude . . ."*

CHAPTER XIX

The Glorious Fourth

"HAPPY holiday, pal!"

For a moment, Rick thought he was at home. Then he sat upright and looked into the face of Scotty, bending over him.

"Hey, why didn't you wake me for my watch?" he demanded.

Scotty grinned. "You looked like you were dreaming of ice cream. I remember we always used to have ice cream on the Fourth of July!"

"Holy smokes!" Rick jumped from his sleeping bag. "This *is* the Fourth of July!"

"Yeah," Scotty said sourly. "Happy Independence Day."

"Only I'm not feeling very independent this morning," Rick remarked. He looked across the plateau at Zircon, still busily pumping away at the key. The big scientist tried to muster a grin and asked, "Where are your fireworks?"

"That would be appropriate, wouldn't it?" Rick said.

"Shall we drop down to the drugstore and get some?"

The reminder of home sobered everyone for a moment and then Scotty spoke up. "Hey, that reminds me. Barby gave us both a package that we were supposed to open today."

Rick started to grin. "Say, do you suppose that little monkey made us a present of . . ." He leaped for the pile of equipment and started searching for the boxes that his sister had presented to them with such ceremony.

"Here's mine," he said finally, "but I don't see yours, Scotty."

"The heck with mine. Open it!"

Rick tore the paper from the box and removed the cover.

"Are they . . . ?"

"They are . . . fireworks!"

It was the first time any of them had laughed in a week, and the plateau rang with their boisterous howls.

Rick finally stopped laughing and looked into the box, and shook his head.

"Well, what did you expect to find, a rope ladder?" Scotty jeered.

"It would have been thoughtful of her. Maybe it's in your box," he answered.

"My box. Ha! I just remembered. My box was among that stuff that Sahmeed walked off with."

"Oh, well," Rick answered, "one six-incher is better than none." He drew one of the red firecrackers from the box and held it high.

"It may be our last Fourth, so why don't we show the Mongols how we celebrate a good, rip-roarin' Fourth back home," he said with false gaiety. He walked toward the edge of the plateau and looked over.

Far below, he could see two of the guards posted by the entrance in the base of the rock.

"As though we needed guarding," he commented.

Scotty's eyes were gleaming. "How good a shot are you?" he asked.

"What do you mean?"

Scotty pointed straight down at one of the dozing guards. "See how his leather armor is pulled away from the back of his neck?"

Rick looked. "Impossible," he said.

"Oh, yeah?" Scotty reached for the firecracker in Rick's hand. "Watch an expert," he chuckled.

Rick held a match while Scotty lit the firecracker, then watched his pal hold it over the edge of the plateau. Scotty squinted for a moment, then let the firecracker go. It started to turn over as it fell, then straightened out and plummeted straight to its target! With a shower of sparks, it went straight down the neck of the man and let go!

The Mongol leaped straight into the air and let out the most fearsome howl Rick had ever heard.

Scotty was convulsed with laughter. Zircon deserted his key, and Weiss hurried to the plateau edge as they realized what the boys had done. They all looked down at the guard, who was digging at the back of his armor and shaking his dagger up at them.

"Brother, if he could get his hands on you," Rick said.

"He seemed to know what it was," Scotty observed.

Weiss spoke up. "You forget," he said, "these people are from the land where firecrackers were invented . . . China. It's an old story to them. A very old story."

They turned from the edge and walked back toward the box of fireworks.

"Well, I for one, don't see any sense in having a nice holiday spoiled, just because we're up here," Rick said, trying to speak lightly.

"Neither do I," Scotty replied. But Rick could tell that the excitement of his bull's-eye shot had worn off and his heart wasn't in it.

If they gave in to the gloom that was enveloping them, Rick realized their imprisonment would be even more of a torture than it was already. Hunger was nipping at his insides and would get worse as the day progressed. None of the others had mentioned being hungry or thirsty but he knew that all of them were. With what passed for a laugh, he reached for the box of fireworks and beckoned Scotty to the edge of the cliff. They tried to amuse themselves by dropping the smaller crackers over the side for a while, but this soon palled on them.

"Seems like a waste of time," Scotty sighed.

"We have nothing *but* time." The moment he said it, Rick knew he had queered any holiday atmosphere left in either of them. They dropped the fireworks to the ground and walked to the radar key over which Weiss was now crouching.

They stood there silently, watching Weiss's fingers tap out the message though every last one of them had lost hope that it would ever reach the outside world.

"If we could only *do something*," Scotty suddenly exploded.

It was not his pal's nerve breaking, Rick knew. Scotty meant that he wanted to go down fighting.

"Look, why don't we make this Fourth of July a real whooper-dooper?" Rick suggested.

"Aw, Rick," Scotty objected.

"I think that's a wonderful idea," Weiss spoke up suddenly, surprising them both.

"So do I!" Zircon added. "What's on your mind, Rick?"

"Well," he began, "here is the field telephone." He reached into the equipment box and lifted it out. "We can use the head of it as a microphone."

Light was dawning on Zircon now. "I see. And you want to attach it to an amplifier and speaker, and really give them a grand explosion."

"Wait," Weiss interrupted. "We were going to use that field telephone for communicating between our radar equipment and our camp . . . when we got there."

"Optimist!" Zircon snorted.

"Sure, let's do it." Scotty was enthusiastic now.

Zircon disengaged the amplifier from the radar equipment and started connecting it to the loudspeaker.

"That means no messages for a while," Weiss said worriedly.

"Let them wait," Zircon laughed recklessly. He seemed to be having as much fun as the two boys now.

Rick connected the makeshift microphone to the amplifier and speaker, and Zircon tied the whole into the wind-driven power supply.

"Good thing this is a ten-inch speaker," Rick grinned. "This is really going to make some noise!"

Weiss was rummaging nervously through the equipment. "I hope this turns out all right," he said.

"They'll never forget this Fourth of July." Zircon smiled. "Light your firecrackers, Rick."

Scotty held the microphone far away from him, and Rick held one of the larger crackers in a pair of pliers and lit it.

They held their ears as the firecracker fizzed. And then it exploded with a roar that startled even the scientists who thought they knew what the effect would be.

The blast rolled from the huge speaker in a thunderous wave that smashed against the rocky walls that imprisoned the Lost City, seeming to gain volume as it bounced from ledge to ledge.

"Look at the Mongols," Scotty said, pointing down.

They looked, and saw terrified faces turned up to them.

"Whoopee! Do it again," Julius Weiss yelled.

They roared with laughter at the little man's sudden

enthusiasm and then Rick said, "Why not make this one a whooper-*whooper*-dooper? Two of them at once!"

Zircon slapped Rick on the back in approval. Rick put two crackers within the jaws of the pliers. This time Scotty stretched his arm almost out of its socket to get away from the blast he knew would come. The fuses crackled as Rick touched the match to them and held the firecrackers toward the microphone.

With a roar, they went off, but the ocean of sound that welled from the speaker wiped the smiles off every face.

For as the reverberations rocketed across the city, they felt an ominous rumble. Rick saw Weiss staring beyond him to the left, and as he whirled around, his heart pounded.

A whole section of the mountain wall was slowly detaching itself from the sheer side and with gathering speed started to slip toward the floor of the valley. Then the side of the mountain disengaged itself completely and with a mighty roar plunged toward the earth.

With horror, Rick realized what they had done. Their Fourth of July celebration had set off a landslide!

They were almost knocked from their feet as one half of the crumbling mountain hurled itself outward and landed with a deafening crash squarely in the Lost City!

CHAPTER XX

Return of the Great Khan

CHOKING clouds of dust rose from the floor of the valley and mushroomed out above the city. Their eardrums were still numbed by the mighty roar of the landslide, and below them they could see nothing through the haze.

Rock was still falling, and Rick breathed thankfulness that they could not see the havoc wrought on the Mongols by their innocently intended celebration.

No one spoke. It was impossible to put their anguish into words. They just stared down into the rising cloud of dust.

Finally Zircon muttered, "I didn't want this to happen. Even to be free."

"And especially since it serves no purpose," Weiss added, almost in a whisper.

Rick looked out over the valley, trying to see the extent of the damage wrought by the landslide. Even the golden tomb of Genghis Khan was obscured, and all that his eyes could find was the wall dividing the living city from the dead.

The dust was slowly settling now and they moved to the edge of the plateau to get a better look. Rick saw running figures and winced as he heard agonized wails from below.

Scotty appeared beside him. "If we could only get down from here now," he said urgently. "No one would even notice."

"But how?" Rick's eyes went to the only exit, which was the trap door. They couldn't hope to get that open. There was no way . . . no . . . Wait! On the trap door were the spools of wire they had taken from the repair kit when they made the windmill.

Scotty saw them at the same time. "Look," he exclaimed.

The same thought was in both their minds. They ran to the spools. Rick picked one up. It was heavy copper, insulated with rubber and fabric.

"It would hold a man's weight," he said.

"Mine," Scotty replied. "Let's get busy."

"Not you," Rick objected. "If anyone takes the chance, I will."

"Let's see your hands."

He held them out, and realized that Scotty was right. He had forgotten that his hands were scored and cut from his descent down the rocks. In the excitement of all that had happened since, he hadn't noticed the pain.

"It's my job," Scotty said. "Come on, help me."

The professors were at their sides now. "Scotty can

get down on the wire," Rick explained quickly, adding to himself: "With luck." It was a terrible risk. The Mongols might see the descending figure. Or the wire might part. It wasn't designed to take such a load. And what could they hitch it to?

Scotty thought it over, then decided. "I'll go down hand over hand. You couldn't lower me. There isn't anything to take a purchase on."

"We'll each wind a coil of the line around our bodies, then lie down and each hold on to one of the crates," Zircon suggested.

Rick almost objected. He didn't want Scotty to take the chance. Then he realized that, for Scotty, it was only a choice of two evils. Stay on the plateau and starve, or try the wire and perhaps survive. If he failed, it would at least be a quick end.

Rick turned hurriedly and walked to the edge of the plateau, while the others unwound coil after coil of the heavy wire. He didn't want Scotty to see how worried he was. Only after he had stood a moment, looking down into the choking clouds of dust that still rose from the valley, did he regain control of his expression and hurry back to help the others join the wires together.

They twisted two wires together to form a stronger line, rechecked the places where they had connected coil to coil. Then, one by one, they shook hands with Scotty.

"You'll make it," Zircon said briefly.

Weiss's smile was confident. "We'll expect you back through the trap door."

Rick took his friend's hand. "Easy does it, fella."

Scotty took a pair of rubberized gloves from the repair kit and slipped them on. "Back in ten minutes," he said calmly.

Zircon, as the heaviest, would be anchor man. He wound the wire around his big body twice, then secured the end firmly. Rick was next in line. He made a double coil right in front of Zircon and slipped into it. In front of him, Weiss did the same. Then they all lay down on their stomachs, feet toward the edge of the plateau, arms around the heaviest crates they could find.

Scotty lowered the wire down the side of the plateau closest to the mountainside and saw that it reached the ground with room to spare. "Hold tight," he warned. "Here I go."

Rick noted that his friend's voice seemed perfectly normal. Again he wondered at Scotty's control, knowing that the boy must be scared stiff. His face was away from the edge, but he knew by the tension on the wire when Scotty put his weight on it, and he knew when Scotty went over the edge because the strands bit cruelly into his middle, and he had to grit his teeth to keep from crying out.

Then he felt himself sliding! The awful realization came to him that Scotty's weight was pulling them all toward the edge!

Rick tried to dig in with his feet and felt the leather soles scrape against the rock. He sank his teeth into his lip with the strain of holding fast to the crate he held, and saw that it was sliding, slowly, relentlessly back.

Behind him, he heard Weiss exclaim, and cold sweat started out on his face. The little professor must be near the edge! In front of him, he could see Zircon's powerful legs pushing against the flat surface, as though the big scientist were trying to swim forward toward the center of the plateau.

The stone scored his elbows and rubbed through the thick fabric of his woolen shirt, but he didn't even feel the pain. Like Zircon, he was trying to hold his ground with swimming motions, driving his legs against the flat stone that gave no grip whatsoever.

How long had it been? Eternity had passed since the wire had bitten into his waist. His breath was ragged with trying to breathe against the constriction, and he felt wetness around his waist that might be blood.

Weiss let out a strangled yell and Rick and Zircon increased their efforts to hold fast. The slow, terrible dragging went on, and his elbows left thin smears of red where they pressed against the stone.

Zircon's breathing was loud, but he heard no further sound behind him. He was afraid to look anywhere but straight ahead. Were they all to drop from the edge?

His kicking feet pushed . . . and met nothing! A horrified gasp was forced from him and his clutching hands pulled at the slowly moving crate.

His feet were already over the edge . . . his ankles . . . his legs were waving uselessly, his knees scraping the rock . . .

The pressure stopped.

Scotty had reached the ground! *Or had the wire parted?*

Rick scrambled back from the edge, feeling the drag of Weiss's body on the wire. Zircon's powerful legs pushed at the rock, and inch by inch, they regained what they had lost, until a weak voice said, "All right. I'm . . . I'm up."

Zircon whipped out of the wire coils and jumped to help Weiss. The little professor tried valiantly to stand, but his knees buckled and he fell flat.

Rick unwound the wire from around his waist, feeling the pain as it came loose. He felt as though he had been cut in half.

Julius Weiss was stark white, even his lips colorless. "He dragged me right over," he said weakly. "I thought . . ."

"I know," Zircon said hoarsely. "I thought we were all done for. Did he make it?"

Rick staggered to the edge and looked down, one hand on his aching midriff. Far below, the dangling wire vanished into the cloud of dust. "I think he must have," he said.

For a few moments none of them spoke, each busy tending his wounds. Rick gulped air into his tortured lungs, inspected the welts where the wire had cut, and found that the wetness was only perspiration. He looked at his raw elbows and knees and winced at the torn, scraped flesh.

Then he went to the opposite side and tried to see through the heavy cloud of dust down to the entrance.

He could see dim shapes in the dust, and knew that the Mongols were at the entrance. Probably some of them had hidden from the avalanche, in the passageway. How could Scotty get through that?

A low rumble jarred the thoughts from him. He looked up, and up, to an overhanging ledge of rock far above the valley floor. He heard Weiss and Zircon gasp behind him, but he couldn't take his eyes from the ledge. Slowly, ever so slowly, it detached from the mountainside and seemed to float down and down.

A grinding roar shook the stone platform and smashed against his eardrums in beating waves. Dust and broken rock erupted high in the air and fell around them in a gravelly rain.

For a full five minutes, the three on the plateau stood with bowed heads, their hands held high to protect them from debris that fell in the wake of the great ledge. The roar slowly lessened and gave way to sharp explosions as small rocks smashed into the valley. Then there was only silence.

Rick looked up, his face pale.

"Please God that's the last of it!" Zircon said.

The dust was all around them now, rising in great gusts up toward the very peaks, coating everything with brown grit and blotting out the sun.

Then, with a suddenness that sent a chill through the travelers, the whole dust-choked valley was bathed in a weird green light.

It spread over their heads in an arc and exploded into colored balls of fire.

"Look," Weiss yelled.

His shaking hand pointed to the high wall that divided the city from the tomb of the Khan.

There, shadowy in the eerie light of the rocket, stood a terrible figure dressed in leather armor and standing with feet wide apart on the wall. It wore a great helmet with a horsetail crest, and on one arm was an embossed shield. From the free hand spurted a fountain of fire that arched into the sky.

The Genghis Khan!

A surprised gasp came from the two professors, and Rick's lips framed the name: "Scotty!"

But the sound was drowned out by the wail that rose from the city below. Through the dust they glimpsed faintly a thousand Mongols, kneeling in abject worship and bowing toward the figure on the wall.

Rick came alive suddenly. "Professor Weiss," he shouted above the wailing. "Get on the mike and tell them the Khan has returned. Tell them to get us down from here. We're the Khan's true messengers! Tell them!"

"He's right," Zircon yelled. "Hurry, Julius!"

Weiss gripped the microphone and began to chant in Mongol. Rick couldn't understand the words, but even to him it sounded impressive. Later, Weiss told him what had been said.

The Great Khan, The Mighty Khan, Ruler Of All Men, has come again! Hear ye, people of the valley, hear and obey! Free my true messengers whom ye have imprisoned on the Hill of the Thousand Repentant An-

cestors! Take them with all their belongings to the valley entrance and set them free, that they may carry news of my coming to the outer world.

The sonorous voice rolled out, echoing hollowly from the rock walls.

This is the word of the Great Khan! OBEY!

A sigh like the rushing of a wind rose from the Mongols. They were prostrated, no man daring to lift his face to the awful being on the wall.

Rick looked again for the figure on the wall. It was gone! Where had Scotty gone?

They waited. The minutes ticked past and no one spoke.

Then the trap door grated and lifted slowly upward!

The head of the young warrior called Subotai appeared. He didn't look at them. Behind were other warriors, eyes downcast.

"We're sacred," Rick whispered. "They're afraid to look."

Hastily, as though in fear of a deadly curse, the warriors lifted the equipment boxes. Zircon, Weiss, and Rick hastily piled loose odds and ends into empty crates. Subotai whacked his warriors with the flat of his sword, urging them to greater speed.

The equipment vanished through the entrance, and in an amazingly short time the plateau was cleared. With a low bow, eyes averted, Subotai stood aside. It was time for them to leave.

The stairs rushed by as they ran down, and then they were outside, breathing the dust-laden air. The city was a shambles, Rick saw. But the crowd of Mongols who bowed down to the earth seemed undiminished. With relief he realized that the place where the avalanche hit must have been thinly populated. Luckily, the slide had given some warning. Few Mongols, if any, had been caught under the mass.

But the one man whom they might have wished ill suddenly shouted and ran toward them.

Henrick Van Groot!

And, behind him, Sahmeed!

"We've got to get out of here," Rick shouted. But as he spoke he saw Van Groot wrenching at his pocket.

He was reaching for a gun!

Rick scooped up a rock and hurled it, all his strength in the throw. It crunched into Van Groot's stomach and doubled him up.

Sahmeed leaped forward, his face contorted.

Zircon was there to meet him.

Rick ran to Van Groot just as the man staggered to his feet, reaching again for the gun in his pocket. Rick bent low, doubling up his fist. All the strength of his wiry body was in the haymaker he swung from his shoe tops. He felt his knuckles crack as the blow landed. Van Groot's legs buckled.

Julius Weiss stepped in and smacked the renegade sharply on the head with the flat of a sword he had picked up. Van Groot tumbled to the ground and was quiet.

Rick whirled, to see Sahmeed and Zircon locked in

a titanic embrace. He grabbed a rock and leaped to the scientist's aid, but his help was not needed.

Zircon brought up his hands sharply against the giant guide's throat, breaking Sahmeed's hold. The guide rocked backward, and, as he did, Zircon's fist came up with all the weight of his big body behind it. The balled fist caught Sahmeed. He kept going backward, with increased impetus, fighting for balance. His heels struck a rock. He catapulted over and his head struck the ground with an audible crack. He lay very still.

"Run," Zircon yelled.

In a moment they caught up with Subotai and the warriors, who were lugging their equipment as fast as their short legs would travel. As the last crate was carried up the steps and into the passageway that led from the valley, Subotai and his men turned and hurried away.

At that moment a mighty roar went up from the city.

"We've been found out," Rick exclaimed. Then he saw Scotty.

The weirdly clad figure that had been on the wall was racing toward them with ground-eating strides. It bounded up the steps and into the passageway.

"Let's go," Scotty shouted.

Out of the dust cloud, half the warriors of the lost city came charging, waving swords. The vanguard knelt and discharged bows. Arrows rattled against the stone.

"Hurry," Scotty said urgently.

From right over their heads came an ominous rumble. The four pushed into the passageway just as rock cascaded down in an ever increasing mass. The roar increased to a thunderous crash and all light was blotted out.

The passageway into the lost city was closed!

"Scotty," Rick choked, "what happened?"

"It was all arranged," Scotty yelled above the din. "Let's get out of here, in case the roof of the tunnel goes."

For the next few minutes no one spoke as they wrestled the equipment to the outer end of the passageway. At last, they stood in the sunlight, breathless from their frantic efforts.

Scotty, attired in his strange garb, grinned at them, but it was a strained grin. "I went in to see what had happened to you, and they saw me. That tipped them off, I guess, because some of them had seen me before."

"But the rockets!" Rick exclaimed. "And the landslide that blocked the entrance . . ."

"I had help," Scotty said. "Unexpected help." His grin broadened.

A familiar voice spoke from the rock ledge above them.

"Happy, joyous Fourth Holiday!"

There, grinning down at them, stood Chahda!

CHAPTER XXI

Success

FOOD had never tasted so good. The four travelers and Chahda sat around a cooking fire stuffing themselves with all the good things their recovered rations afforded. They paused between mouthfuls only long enough to answer or ask questions.

Scotty fished a can of hamburger out of the fire and opened it, explaining meanwhile: "I didn't know whether my weight was pulling you all after me, or whether it was the wire stretching, but I didn't want to take any chances, so when I got near enough to the ground, I just let go."

"A good thing you did!" Rick said. "Professor Weiss was already over, and my legs were kicking in space. I was plenty scared, brother!"

Weiss stopped sipping hot tea long enough to add: "I cried out when I slipped over, but then I decided I was practically dead and nothing could save me. Being pulled back up again was like a miracle."

"There were plenty of miracles," Scotty said. "I ran

around the plateau and bumped right into a whole platoon of warriors. They didn't notice me, I guess, because by that time I was so coated with dust that they couldn't tell I wasn't one of them. But I saw that it wasn't any use trying to get into the hill. The passageway was blocked with Mongols, all hiding from the landslide."

"We guessed as much," Zircon nodded.

"They were all bowing and praying like crazy," Scotty continued. "That was what gave me the idea of playing Genghis Khan. I skinned back through the city as fast as I could leg it. For a while, I couldn't figure out how I was going to get over the wall, then I saw a tree right next to it. I shinned up the tree, and it bent over like a birch, and there I was on the wall. After that it was easy. I jumped down and ran to the Golden Tomb. We'd looked around before they caught us, so I knew right where the armor and stuff was. And, while I was getting into it . . ."

"Chahda comes," the Hindu boy beamed.

"And how." Scotty grinned. "With my box of fireworks that I left on the yak."

"I have hear the noise," Chahda explained. "I can see you on the rock making shoots with firecracks. So I am thinking: 'I will make the shoots, too, and you will know that Chahda is here.' But when I am come back with the box, there is Sahib Scotty!"

"It's a good thing Scotty left his box of fireworks with the caravan," Rick said. "Those Roman candles made quite some effect, believe me. For a minute I thought it was old Genghis himself."

"Chahda's arrival was little short of miraculous," Zircon remarked. "I, for one, never expected to see the caravan again. Or Sahmeed," he added, smiling with satisfaction at the memory of that encounter.

Chahda accepted a second helping of bacon and eggs. "Is most short, my story," he said. "I am wake up when Sahmeed is talking soft to the bearers. He is say to them: 'You come with me quiet like mouses or maybeso I make the break on the neck, you bet!'

"I am almost waking up you, but I am think: 'If I am waking, maybe there is fight and the Sahibs is hurt.' So I go with Sahmeed to Nepal, and I am tell the police and we are coming back for you."

"We figured that was what you had planned," Rick said.

"Is so," Chahda agreed. "But when a day is going by, Sahmeed says to us: 'You waits here. I am go get many rupees for us. Soon we be much rich. So you wait. I come back two, three days.'"

Weiss nodded. "He wanted to get back to the lost city and contact Van Groot. I imagine he was afraid of not getting his money. Do you suppose any of the other bearers knew about the city?"

"They not know." Chahda shook his head. "Sahmeed not telling us. But when he is go, I am talking to bearers. I am saying: 'How we know Sahmeed is coming back? This Sahmeed, he is much bad one. He not giving us rupees. You want rupees, you come with me. The Sahibs will give much rupees. More than Sahmeed.'"

The Hindu boy paused to take a sip of tea. "They talk much, those men. They say to me: 'How we know the Sahibs give much rupees?' I am answer: 'How you know Sahmeed come back? Also, you do not go to the Sahibs, soon is coming police to put you from jail.' They listen, and they think I speak good. So we come back."

"But we weren't there," Rick said.

"Is true. We hunt very long, and we climb hills and look some more, and then one man is seeing green jacket way high on mountain. I look, and I think maybe belongs Sahib Rick. So we hunt near there, and we are finding yak. He is near hole in mountain. I go in, and what I see!"

"Sahmeed must have already been in the city by then," Weiss guessed.

"I think Sahmeed, he is maybe Mongol," Chahda said.

"He looks like one," Rick agreed. "But I don't think he's one of the Mongols from the city."

"There are many Mongols in this area," Zircon said. "They've been pretty well absorbed by the native population, but now and then one comes across the mountains from China. Likely, Sahmeed got to Nepal that way. I imagine Van Groot met him when he first left the lost city, and hired him on the spot. They were certainly two of a kind."

"It would have done your heart good to see Professor Zircon smack that big hulk square on the chin.

I'll bet it jarred him loose from his mustache," Rick told Scotty.

"I'd like to have seen you swat Van Groot, too," Scotty grinned.

"Well, we needn't worry about either of them any longer," Rick gestured toward the sealed entrance of the city. "They're in there now, and to stay."

"You still haven't told us how you managed that last landslide," Zircon prompted.

"Well, I figured we might need some kind of rear guard," Scotty explained. "So when I met Chahda, I told him to beat it back to the entrance and get some of the bearers and climb up the mountainside. When we first got into the city I noticed there was a sheer cliff on the inner side, but the outside of the tunnel could be climbed."

Chahda picked up the tale. "I get three mens, and we climb far up, and there is a little place where we can squeeze in, so we do, and when we come out the other side, there is the city. And we look down and we can see the steps which is going in the city from the passage. I look good, and I find a big stone which is loose. We wait, long time. Soon comes you. Then comes Sahib Scotty, and there is many Mongols behind, so I think: 'Is now, Chahda!' We push the big stone and bang! Much more stone is falling."

"It's a good thing rock slides easily in this country," Rick said.

"That's the strange part of it," Zircon observed. "Actually, it shouldn't. But I have a theory that this part of

Tibet, or at least this immediate area, was under water at one time. The result is this type of rock, a kind of shale."

Scotty scratched his head. "But you wouldn't think just a firecracker explosion would blast it loose."

"That is understandable," Weiss put in. "By the time the explosion was amplified, it was far beyond a mere firecracker noise. Then, with the sound hemmed in by the valley walls, there was a great deal of reverberation —which means that the vibration on loose stone must have been very great. You've seen pictures of glaciers breaking off when a boat blows its whistle? The effect was similar. And very fortunate for us, too!"

"And unfortunate for Van Groot," Rick added. "He's in there now, and I don't know how he'll get out."

"A lot of good his pitchblende will do him," Scotty agreed.

"The Tibetan government must know about that," Zircon said. "And about this Mongol city. We will have to see that they are notified."

"They be very happy," Chahda said. "Is most poor country, this Tibet. I read this in Worrold Alm-in-ack."

Zircon smiled at the boy. "And how are we going to repay you, Chahda?"

"Is most easy." Chahda smiled. "When you take me to 'Merica, is good payment, I think!"

The four travelers looked at each other, grinning.

"He's certainly earned his passage," Rick said.

The others nodded.

"I don't know how we'll arrange it," Zircon bellowed, "but you're as good as in America right now, young man!"

Silence fell over the group as they completed their meal. Rick wondered: Now what? Only three days remained until the tenth. Their equipment was intact, barring the loss of the batteries Van Groot had taken, but they could never reach Tengi-Bu on time, even with the bearers and yaks.

"It seems a shame to go through so much trouble," he said, "and then not be ready to transmit on time."

"I've been giving that some thought," Zircon said. "Julius, have you any ideas?"

"There are a great many factors to consider, Hobart," the little professor replied thoughtfully. "First, we are actually close enough to Tengi-Bu so that the angle of transmission will not be seriously affected." He waved an arm at the encircling mountains. "But how could we hope to get a signal out of this pocket?"

"We did on the plateau, didn't we?" Scotty pointed out.

The professors smiled. "No," they said in unison, and then grinned at each other.

Zircon explained. "Our message never got out, Scotty. The power was too weak even to activate the modulator. Julius knew it, I was sure. But I felt that doing something, even something futile, would help our morale."

"Quite so," Weiss agreed. "Hobart, if we could find

a suitable location near at hand, perhaps on top of one of these near-by peaks, we could very possibly set up in time."

"Provided ground conditions were right," Zircon agreed. "Well, there is no point in worrying about it now. I propose we get a good night's sleep and then start hunting. Fortune has smiled on us, gentlemen. I don't believe she'll let us down now."

It was Rick who finally located a suitable transmission point. He went back over his memories of the climb down the mountainside before he had found the lost city, and recalled seeing a near-by peak that looked very much like the Hill of the Thousand Repentant Ancestors.

Then the problem was to locate the peak. He and Scotty climbed back up the mountainside toward the place where his jacket still rested—and would certainly remain until the elements rotted it away—and spotted the peak a few miles south of their present location.

By nightfall, the professors and the three boys had scouted the location, found a gradual slope that led to the top, and had pitched camp, the bearers following with the equipment and supplies.

Only two days remained until the tenth.

They were busy days. The equipment had to be set up and tested, water and fuel had to be carried for the steam-powered generator. While Scotty and some of the bearers hunted for fuel, Rick and others of the group searched for water. Finally they found a spring that flowed in a crevice between two peaks. And then the water had to be hauled up laboriously in a bucket on a rope.

But at last the equipment was ready, except for supply voltage for the tube filaments. This was Weiss's problem. He ransacked the spare-parts kit and finally rigged up a workable rectifier that would transform power from the big generator to the proper direct-current voltage.

Not until the predawn hours of July tenth was everything ready and the radar transmitter tested.

Rick was helping Professor Zircon make final adjustments on the big, oblong antenna when Scotty came up. "The generator's turning over," he reported. "It's half past five."

A queer little chill ran down Rick's spine. Six o'clock was the time set for the trial. From their high peak he looked out across the Tibetan mountains. To the east was a faint glow, heralding the coming of daylight, but the valleys below were still inky with darkness.

In the west, the moon was slowly dipping toward the horizon. He knew that on the other side of the world, at Spindrift Island, it was nearing eight o'clock in the evening of the previous day, July 9th. And the moon would be rising out of the sea, and his father and mother, and Barby, and the professors . . . yes, even Dismal . . . would be watching it and thinking of the little group in faraway Tibet.

Rick swallowed the sudden lump in his throat and hurried over to Julius Weiss, who was checking the instruments, while Chahda looked on.

"A constant four-forty volts," Weiss said. "Good. Hobart, will you take a look at the plate readings?"

In a circle around the equipment, the bearers were gathered, eyes wide, watching the final preparations.

As the minutes ticked away, Rick shivered a little from excitement as well as the early morning chill. To the east, streaks of light were sharply silhouetting the mountains.

"Six o'clock," Zircon called in a ringing voice.

Weiss opened his transmitter key, and there was the rapid click of the contact points as he tapped.

Tibet relay calling Spindrift . . .

Before the message was fully out, the radar scope broke into points of green light, and harsh code from the speaker mingled with the sound of Weiss's key.

Rick's eyes were glued to the scope. That was their own message that activated the scope and the speaker like a badly timed echo. It had already gone to the moon and returned, traveling the 326,000-mile round trip through space in slightly less than two seconds. At this very moment, Hartson Brant and the others would be receiving the message "bounce" at Spindrift, just as they were receiving it here!

The signals died. The scope was quiet again, and the speaker gave forth only a faint humming.

Seconds ticked by. Would Spindrift answer? Had that echo to Weiss's message really returned from the moon, or from the high mountains close by?

Zircon let out a bellow of delight.

The scope was flickering, and from the speaker the

Morse code came over, loud, clear explosions of sound . . .

Spindrift calling Tibet relay via luna . . . we read you loud and clear . . .

Then they were all shouting at once and shaking hands, and the bearers watched, awed by this miracle they did not understand.

"It's our turn now . . ." Zircon began.

"Wait!" said Weiss. "There's more."

Again the crackling code.

Greetings to you all. Is all well?

Rick's eyes went to the mountain wall that hid the Lost City. Yes, all was well—now.

The messages would go back and forth, checking technical data, antenna settings, and so on, but the important thing was that the lunar relay had worked!

"Anything we want to tell the folks back home?" Zircon asked.

"Yes!" Rick exclaimed. "Yes!"

The others grinned their approval and Chahda beamed as Rick said:

"Tell Barby thanks for the fireworks!"